THE SPIDER:
HORDES OF THE RED BUTCHER

THE **MASTER** OF **MEN** !

SPIDER®

HORDES OF
THE RED BUTCHER

By Grant Stockbridge

STEEGER BOOKS • 2020

CHAPTER 1
ATTACK IN THE NIGHT

RICHARD WENTWORTH was thrown forward in his Pullman seat as, beneath him, steel flanges screeched and the Dixie Limited braked to an emergency stop. Up ahead, the locomotive's whistle belched frantic yelps into the thick darkness, then chopped off like a woman throttled in the middle of a scream. The lights went out.

In the sudden darkness, men and women cried out, shouting questions. Their voices held incipient panic. Not absolute terror; just fright and surprise. The lights were out, the train was bucking to an emergency stop—but it was still on the tracks; they were not terrified... yet.

Before anyone else in the car recovered from the lurch, Wentworth had already raced its length and come out on the steel platform. His lips pressed, hard and cold, against his teeth. His hands tapped the bulge of the heavy automatic beneath each arm. Then he unfastened and swung open the right-hand door. His breathing was slightly roughened, but not from exertion.

If other passengers discovered what even he only dimly guessed, their shouts would hold more than mild. They would shriek with a soul-destroying panic akin to insanity! But they did not know... yet.

Without lifting the platform-cover of the steps, Wentworth stood peering out into the lowering darkness. The train had

now shuddered to a complete halt, and the great headlight was out. But he could see, beside the tracks, a low clay bank slanting upward, its crest crowned in dense underbrush, and, beyond, the woods and the dark irregular mass of the Kentucky hills.

From the locomotive came impatient hissings of steam. Far ahead, lurid light colored the sky, a red glow which brightened, then dimmed, with a slow, mighty rhythm. *Fire!*

But that was the only movement. And the gabbling of voices,

confused footsteps behind him, the only sounds. The sustained quiet was unnatural. It was pregnant and awful....

And then, through it, tore a scream. Clearly, terribly, with a rising shrillness quivering on the jagged edge of madness, a woman screamed.

Coldness raced over Wentworth's body. A curse caught in his throat. While the scream still sounded, he leaped across the platform, wrenched at the other door, swung it inward with a squeal of reluctant hinges, and sprang out into the track-side of the ditch. There he crouched, a gun already in his hand.

The coldness, which had stayed with him, suddenly crawled up and down his spine with the torment of a torturer's iron. For the line of coaches was silhouetted blackly against the crimsoned sky—and what he saw, clinging to the side of the car ahead, hunched sharply against the lighter background, confirmed his fears as nothing else could possibly have confirmed them! That bestial, hairy thing....

The village of Horton, quivering under the horror of four ghastly murders in one night, not to mention the looting of its small but wealthy bank, had reported strange beasts roaming its streets. That report had brought Wentworth westward, although newspapers had laughed and other cities had—figuratively—put derisive tongues in their cheeks. And here, now, some bestial monster hung to the side of the coach clutching a woman who screamed....

WENTWORTH LIFTED his automatic deliberately. As he did so, the queer hunched thing bounded down into the ditch with the woman, still screaming, dangling over its shoulder. A single giant leap, and it had cleared the ditch, lumbered into the underbrush, and was gone.

Wentworth had not been able to shoot. Woman and monster had merged to one blurred, featureless mass in the darkness. Now both were gone. Only the screams, fearful in the thick night, marked the going.

Mad thoughts hurled themselves against his brain as he

4

sprang up the clay embankment and with long powerful strides flung through the underbrush. Intent only on pursuit, he did not see two vaguely bestial shadows rise to right and left of his path and creep forward....

Not that the sight would have stopped him. A lesser man would have fled in frantic terror at the first glimpse of that hairy shape. But Richard Wentworth, secretly the Spider, had come from New York for this very battle! He was the champion of oppressed humanity, its shield and protector against the murderous outbreaks of the Underworld; wherever crime struck terribly that way he hastened, taking up the challenge.

His exploits had raised him to the proportions of a legendary hero. In ancient days, Rome would have made him an emperor-god. Salem might have burned him as a sorcerer. The modern world—well, the police had offered rewards totaling thousands of dollars for his capture "dead or alive." And the Underworld hated him and plotted his destruction with a fierceness bred of abject terror.

But the Spider was indifferent alike to proscription by the Underworld and dogged persecution by police. Evading their bullets and traps, he continued to fight his thankless battle as humanity's paladin—a campaign which now had brought him to Kentucky. His keen mind had recognized truth in the reports of "strange beasts" seen in the streets of a certain country town, had recognized unutterable menace in the four horrible murders which had attended the looting of the town bank....

These thoughts came back to him as he raced in the wake of the screaming woman. In spite of his speed, the beast-thing was distancing him with its great bounding leaps through the shrubbery. Still unconscious of the two shadows that lurked in ambush, Wentworth lengthened his stride. His fists tightened about the butts of his automatics.

Then a flicker in the darkness to his left caught his keen eyes. With a quickness only his super-trained muscles could have achieved, Wentworth deliberately tripped himself, sprawling with fearful force into the tangle of shrubbery. Over his head whickered the missile he had glimpsed, making a hoarse whining sound as it passed.

Half stunned by the violence of his fall, he clung to his guns with the instinct of a drowning man. Having landed in a ball, he was crouching on his feet within split seconds after hitting the ground.

Against the sky, he was able to make out the hunched, massive shoulders of the beast which had attacked him. He flung a swift glance about—and spotted a second huge shape creeping in on his right….

A MIRTHLESS smile twisted Wentworth's lips. His breath came lightly through clenched teeth. The screams ahead were changed now; pain blended with terror. Desperately he fought to remain motionless, until he could make sure of his shots at these two. His mind flicked to the missile which had whined overhead and he remembered the reports on the four men who had died so horribly in the streets of Horton three nights before….

One had been the lone policeman who patrolled the streets. He had been killed instantly yet in a way doctors still were unable to fathom. Wentworth could recall the coroner's findings: "If a bullet two inches across had been shot into the victim's body at close range, from a gun of extraordinary power, it might have created such a wound."

The bullet—if it had been a bullet—had ploughed completely through the body, taking with it the heart, leaving a gaping hole tunneled from back to chest. Yet no one had heard a shot. The watchman of the bank had died similarly, and two boys, returning late from a neighboring town, had been found in the shattered wreckage of their car, one of them with his skull actually pulped.

Even the coroner's report displayed a note of horror: "The blow was so violent that it fractured every vertebra down to the fifth. I cannot convey any idea of its force. The skull must have been pulped instantly—yet the blow was terrific enough to fracture also the tough fiber of the vertebrae, which thus were *not hit directly.*"

Wentworth knew now that the things which had killed those four had been missiles hurled by these beastlike creatures, hurled with such force as to drive entirely through a man's body, pulp his skull! Such a missile as he himself had just dodged. His muscles tensed as he realized the strength which must lurk in the massive shoulders of these two things now creeping upon him. A gorilla might well lose a hand to hand conflict with such as these....

Ahead, in the darkness, the woman's shrieking pain changed to hysterical, sobbing laughter. Then that as well choked off with

a horrible suddenness. Intoler-
able silence set in.

Abruptly it was broken by
a hollow thumping, as if from
a huge, muted drum. Then a
hoarse scream echoed through
the night. A hoarse, triumphant scream, half human—
and half beast!

In the very midst of it, the
two massive things in the
brush closed in on Wentworth.

HE FORCED himself to remain motionless even yet, waiting
for them. Waiting while from the train, too, came frantic shouts
of suffering and fright.

His breath issued raggedly through his open mouth, his heart
was pounding high and hard, but he gripped his automatics with
hands as steady as rocks.

Overhead the clouds were low and thick, around him a small
cold wind wandered about the shrubbery, rustling leaves impatiently. The wind was more noisy than the two creeping beasts.

But the creatures were near enough now. At a range of fifteen
feet Wentworth lifted his left gun deliberately and fired at the
beast on that side.

The blast and flash of fire wiped out all other senses for an
instant and during it he sprang two long strides ahead, then
crouched again. A bestial roar of pain had come from the creature he had hit, the roar was answered from the right, and with a

8

monstrous thrashing of shrubbery both beasts charged in upon the spot he had just vacated.

He felt himself frowning as he lifted his automatic again. His aim, developed through long years of practice, was unswervingly accurate whether he fired on a well lighted target or, in a thick smother of blackness, at another weapon's flash. In fact the very roar of the beast told him he had registered a hit. Yet, with a .45 bullet in its body, the thing came on!

His second blast exploded when the creature was no more than ten feet away, and his leftward spring was barely an instant ahead of a double attack. At one leap, together, the beastlike things covered the next ten feet and he felt the earth quiver with the fury of their blows as they flailed at the shrubbery with crushing weapons.

A sense of utter unreality gripped Wentworth. Twice he had pumped bullets unerringly into the body of that bestial monstrosity, and twice the thing had felt their effect so little that it could strike with a force to shake the ground! Quivering dread raced through Wentworth's brain. The two beasts were making filthy mouthings of rage. Their blows thudded with incredible rapidity. Sparks flew high as the weapon of one struck a rock.

Wentworth lifted both guns. But, with weapons leveled, he hesitated. He was a scant two yards from where the creatures stood; a distance they could cover in lightning speed. Two of his bullets had failed even to slow one of the monsters....

Slowly, tensely, he moved backward. He hated himself for retreating—and yet, if bullets, even bullets, could not stop them....

At a distance of fifteen feet, he again lifted his automatics. His body was hard with tension, his lips curled back from even teeth. Something primitive was stirring in him, something primitive like a child's fear of the dark. But he fought down its black writhings and began to squeeze both triggers. The guns leaped in his hands and the blasts of their lightning flashed through the low shrubbery.

THE ABSENCE of gun recoil first registered on his senses the fact that he had emptied his guns. Ahead of him, shrubbery tore apart, fierce roaring shook the sky. Once more the two beasts charged!

With a smothered cry Wentworth turned and ran toward the train. As he ran, hard, bitter curses squeezed out between his teeth. He thrust one automatic into his holster and with jerking hands managed to reload the other.

Anger was surging within him now, fighting his instinctive flight before the uncanny vitality of those bullet-pierced beasts. There was nothing like them in the catalogue of modern zoology: that he knew. Furthermore, beasts did not loot banks after killing the guards. They would not know how to stop a train hurtling through the night. If these things were indeed the beasts they appeared to be, there was a human agency behind them! At the thought, rage swept Wentworth.

With a curse that was almost a shout, he whirled about to face the things. Their crashing was farther away than he had any right to hope it would be. He crouched low, but he could not outline them against the blackness of the woods. And gradually, unbelieving, he realized that instead of following, they were retreating toward the thick trees.

His anger urged him to plunge back after them. But with a tension that made his legs quiver, he held himself in check. His fingers mocked him with their steadiness as he swiftly reloaded his second gun and turned toward the train.

Suddenly he realized that not a sound was issuing from where the dark bulk of the Dixie Limited stood motionless upon the rails. Up ahead the flickering red glow still played against the clouds, but it was dying. That was the only motion—and the only sound in all the vicinity was his own hoarse breathing.

Then a vagrant wind made little scurryings in the leaves about his thighs. In the ditch beside the tracks, a cricket began an experimental chirp. And after it a whole chorus of night insects picked up the sounds. In the distance, a hound bayed desolately.

With furious apprehension, Wentworth stumbled forward. He was afraid to discover the meaning of that silence. His guns hung like lead in his hands—while the thin cheerless rasp of the crickets mocked him ironically. At the brink of the clay embankment beside the tracks he paused. Gropingly, he dragged out a small flashlight, sprayed its light below. The next instant a sickened curse escaped his tortured lips.

There were two bodies down there. A man, who lay on his back, with a raw stump where his head *had* been, from which shreds of flesh dangled. He had been beheaded, but not with any edged weapon. His head had been torn from his shoulders! And beside the man, a girl. A girl with the fragments of

11

her own clothing strewn about her poor naked body. She had suffered before a merciful blow had smashed her head to a pulp.

Seeing, Wentworth's whole body trembled. A burning flush swept through him, and his hands clenched achingly on his guns. The whole train—he forced the thought into his mind—*the whole train* would be like these two pitiful bodies: a gory shamble.

And a human agency, some ruthless criminal mind, had led these beasts to perpetrate such horrors! Beasts could kill and maim, but beasts could not have stopped the limited.

Presently his trembling left him. He became rigid with a white hot rage. His head wrenched back and he hurled hoarse, rasping curses at the sky. He lifted a gun against the red glimmer dying up ahead. If there was a God above, *the Spider would avenge!*

CHAPTER 2
THE DESERTED VILLAGE

A BITTER energy filled Wentworth. Springing down into the ditch he raced at a pounding run toward the dying fire up ahead. He knew that he ran past dozens of bodies, past unspeakable horrors recorded in blood and worse. But he waited to inspect none of those. He must get help and take the trail of these bestial things which defied the heaviest bullets, which slew by fiendish and herculean strength....

The breath was whistling in his throat when he pelted up to where flames still ate hungrily through the collapsed beams of a railway station. Up the long, deserted street other fires danced over the ruins of five more buildings. No living soul moved there. No sound existed save the hiss and sputter of the flames.

The night was close and hot and seemed to press physically upon his spirit. He dragged a palm across his sweat-beaded forehead, strode vigorously up the street. The doors and windows of undamaged houses were shut tightly, but he sensed, behind them, a furtive activity. He stood in the middle of the street and anger gripped him anew, so that he shook a fist at the closed doors.

"Come out, cowards!" he shouted. "There's no danger now."

Dead silence. Then an echo floated back mockingly. "…*now….*"

Jerkily he strode up the street, passing under the cold white light of arc-lamps. There was anger in the swing of his square shoulders, determination in the taut set of his jaws. His very body radiated a resurgent vitality. He wore no hat and the crisp black crown of his hair emphasized the high intelligence of his forehead. Shadows touched his sensitive, slightly arrogant mouth, but even in the darkness beneath his brows, his gray-blue eyes showed cold burning lights.

If furtive men watched him from barricaded windows, at least no one attempted to halt his march up the middle of the dusty street.

Before the stone-walled county jail he paused once more to shout a challenge, and once more the echo was his only answer. He strode on to the hotel. A great plate glass window had been smashed from it, and a battered wooden door closed the breach.

Wentworth threw his shoulder against the barrier and it wavered. Inside there was an excited exclamation—and then a deep voice boomed a challenge.

"I got a gun on you," it declared. "Don't make no sudden move!"

Wentworth cursed. "Open the door, fool!" He lifted his hands shoulder high. "Come on, hurry!"

The battered door eased aside an inch and eyes looked out—a cold blue human eye, and the black eye of a revolver's muzzle.

Wentworth fought down his rage. In a voice with which he battled vainly to conceal his anger, he explained what had happened. The door was shoved aside then and the man with the revolver disclosed himself. He was powerfully built, rangy and tall, though with labor—stooped shoulders. His hard blue eyes were slitted in a face burned to the color of tanned leather and the gun at his side was lightly but competently held.

WENTWORTH STALKED past him with a single withering glance and caught up a telephone. Within moments he had notified railway headquarters and state police in neighboring towns what had occurred. Then he turned to regard anew the hillsman. The fellow was crouched against the closed barrier now—and all at once he was haranguing someone else outside.

Wentworth strode toward him, his lean face set, his feet hitting the floor hard.

"Either let the man in, or let me out."

The hillsman turned a slow, deliberate head. He spat into a brass cuspidor and dragged the back of his hand against his straw-colored, tobacco-stained mustache.

"You go out," he said flatly.

Once outside, Wentworth confronted a man whose breadth of shoulder made him seem the shorter of the two, though actually they were nearly of a size.

Glancing toward the low-swung Hispania Suiza roadster parked before the hotel, Wentworth said: "You made good time, Jackson. I walked into the middle of this thing here."

Jackson stood stiffly at attention, a soldier every inch of his length. His face was built on the same broad plan as his body: blue eyes, set wide and level; jaws bulging with knots of muscle. These two had served together in France and Jackson had refused a commission in order to continue serving as Wentworth's sergeant.

"I saw the signs, Major," he said, using the wartime title he preferred. "Miss Nita caught me by telephone at the last town. Paducah, sir. Things are going fast in New York, too."

Wentworth tensed. If his sweetheart, Nita van Sloan, had intercepted Jackson in his trip to Kentucky, something important must be happening in New York. Without words, he gestured for the other to continue.

"Miss Nita urges your return at the first possible moment, sir." Jackson spoke in his characteristic flat, Texan drawl. "There's been a series of murders. No motive known. The murderer cuts off a man's head and runs off with it. Two heads have been tossed through the windows of police stations."

Wentworth's brows creased in a vertical frown. "But why? Decapitation—that seems absolutely ridiculous!"

"No one seems to know, Major," Jackson replied. "The new commissioner, Flynn, talks about crazy men."

Wentworth jerked his hand in an impatient gesture. "Crazy men don't bother to toss heads into police stations."

He stood very straight: a hard lean figure with a head which seemed arrogantly poised even when he bowed it as he did now. "It occurs to me," he went on slowly, "that there must be a connection between what happened here and those murders in New York. It isn't reasonable for two series of brutal crimes to break out simultaneously in widely separated parts of the country—and for both sets of crimes to lack motive. There must be a keen, murderous intelligence behind both…" He broke off. "Get a plane ready in Paducah by tomorrow noon. Send a wire to Miss Nita."

The grating of the door behind him pulled Wentworth's head about and he watched a half dozen men file out of the hotel, the mustached hillsman in the lead. They carried rifles at the ready and the leader had the heavy revolver in his right hand.

A slight hard smile touched Wentworth's lips. "So you got over being scared?" he asked shortly.

"We ain't afeered of nothing human," said the leader in a nasal drawl. "We're agoin' now to get the sheriff to deputize a posse."

Wentworth nodded. "Jackson, get a room and stay at the

hotel. Make the arrangements I told you about. Gentlemen, I'll go with you."

THEY STALKED on together, walking in the middle of the dusty street. A few timid lights showed now behind barricaded windows. A cold, prodding wind had started up, and sent dust-whorls scurrying blackly ahead. Flames quivered lightly over the ruins they had destroyed.

As the hillsman stamped onto the porch of the county jail the door flew open and a wild-eyed youngster reeled out, revolver in hand.

"Where are they?" he gasped. "W-where are they?"

The leader cursed. Stepping forward he swung a fist from his knees. The youth hit the wall with a crash, rolled over, and fell on his face.

"What's the idea?" Wentworth demand sharply.

The hillsman spat into the darkness, then dragged the back of his hand across his mustaches.

"That there," he drawled, "is our sheriff."

"You hadn't oughta done that, Welver," one of the other men muttered. "You'd oughta heered what Sheriff Conley had to say, first."

Wentworth rolled the sheriff over on his back, and massaged his neck with deft hard fingers. The man's head rolled laxly. By the rays of a near street light, Wentworth saw now that his first impression of extreme youth here had been wrong. Merely, there was a certain open frankness about the sheriff's face, even with eyes closed, which made it seem almost boyish. Though the way the black hair lay upon his white, high forehead may have added to the impression too.

The sheriff stirred, thrust up on stiff arms—and suddenly was upright, leveling his revolver. For a moment he stood rigidly, obviously fighting a desire to use the weapon. Then he shoved it inside his belt.

"I'm asking you why you hit me, Welver." His voice quivered tensely.

Welver spat again, and stared without words.

Now don't get riled, Ron," someone remarked. "Welver was just hasty."

Welver exploded. "Hasty, hell. When an ordinary cur of a Conley hides out in the jail when it's his bounden duty to protect us…" He halted, stared harder at young Sheriff Ron Conley. The rifle butt rasped as he caught it up from the floor. "Where's Beth?" he whispered. "Damn your yellow Conley soul, *where's Beth?*"

The spasm of pain which crossed the young man's face was genuine, that much Wentworth could see. And the way he swallowed painfully as he tried to speak, shook his head, then gulped out words.

RICHARD WENTWORTH

"Beth was with me when the… the things came," he said. "I put her in the jail to keep her safe. Started back. Something came through the window and knocked me cold. When I came to… Beth… was gone. The beast things got her!"

With an inarticulate snarl Welver jerked his rifle toward

Conley's breast. But Wentworth's fist moved more quickly. The force of his blow spilled Welver in an abrupt heap. The rifle made a loud clatter on the floor.

"This is no time for personal quarrels," Wentworth said sternly. "We've already wasted time while these two argued. Conley, we've got to trail those beast things and do it fast. Can you follow a trail, or get dogs?"

Conley was looking down at Welver. "I can follow a trail," he said slowly. He rolled his shoulders forward as if adjusting a burden to their broad strength. *"Beth!"* he whispered. He almost staggered back through the doorway.

ANOTHER HILLSMAN bent over Welver. "You can't blame Welver," he muttered. "His daughter Beth's been going with Conley after he told her to cut it out. Now Conley lets her get took by one of them damned beast things... Welver hated Conley's father afore him. Father was sheriff until somebody got him. Rifle in the laurel...."

The monotony of the man's voice was a thin thread. Sheriff Ron Conley came back out the doorway with a rifle in each hand. Wentworth took one.

"Beth is either dead," Wentworth said steadily, "or she's being carried off into the hills. The sooner we find out which, the better."

Conley nodded slowly. His face was thin and white beneath the tan. Wentworth saw now that the young fellow was more powerfully built than a first glance had indicated. His chest was deep, and at each full breath strained against the tight texture of his shirt. Wide shoulders, sagging a little now, tapered to narrow hips and sturdy, horse-bowed legs.

"Reckon you're right," he said in a slow soft voice. "We can get horses down at the stable."

He stalked off, Wentworth and a close group, all of whom carried rifles, at his heels. Welver being still unconscious, one man stayed behind to work over him.

"Better to leave him anyway," Wentworth advised coldly. "We can't afford to fight among ourselves." No one answered. No one said anything at all as they got horses at the livery stable, saddled them, and started at a rapid trot across the railroad tracks, into the thick underbrush which crowded against the right-of-way. Saddles creaked, bits jangled when a horse tossed its head.

"I know where one of them killed a woman," Wentworth said slowly. "We could pick up the trail there." He felt young Conley tense beside him and added: "It was a woman from the train."

The men followed him into the darkness, and the sound of their horses stayed close.

"I found out what hit me," said Ron Conley dully. "It was a funny looking stone, long and round, a dull point at each end. It bounced off a window-sill and hit me on the chest. My head hit the floor and that knocked me cold."

Wentworth felt an immense surprise as he listened to the description of rock. About him, no one else voiced a word. The woods were close at hand; even now they were passing over the spot where he had battled the two things with futile bullets.

"The rock," Wentworth said tightly. "It would weigh about ten or twelve pounds perhaps?"

"About that," Conley agreed.

Wentworth frowned. He glanced about, then pulled up his horse and dropped to the ground, spraying light from his flash upon the graveled earth. Brownish spots were spattered about. He drew in a deep breath.

"I wounded one of them," he said. "This trail shouldn't be hard to follow."

Jostling forward, the men sat their saddles in a silent, dark circle. A horse, scenting the blood, jerked its head and blew noisily. One of the men swung down and lighted an oil lantern against the rising wind. Thereafter he walked ahead, following the spots of blood, while the others trailed the swaying beams cast by the lantern.

"What did you ask about the rock for?" Conley queried presently.

Wentworth replied slowly. "What you described is a throwing stone, such as was used by stone age men of twenty—thirty thousand years ago."

"Thirty thousand…" Conley's voice sounded high and shaken. But he paused on the very point of resuming, as the man with the lantern ran back shouting hoarsely.

"Up there among the trees," he cried. "A woman…."

"The woman from the train," Wentworth said quickly.

He pushed his horse ahead and, catching up the lantern, gazed down at the pitiful thing whose suffering, dying screams he had heard.

Her head had been twisted from her shoulders. She was naked.

CHAPTER 3
LAIR OF THE BEAST

WENTWORTH'S RAGE had exhausted him, but he felt his muscles contract. There was a cold certainty within him that he would kill, and kill terribly, when he found the human monsters behind this outrage.

Nor did he mean the bestial men who actually had perpetrated the deed. If they, as he was suspecting now, were some strange freak of preserved atavisms, or throw-backs to prehistoric times, they were not to be too deeply blamed. They killed and maimed; still, that was only their habit and nature....

But the criminal who was behind their activities, behind the decapitations in New York... Vengeful rage returned to him. By God, the Spider would wreak a vengeance!

He stared at the earth and saw, in the dust, two great tracks of naked human feet. Feet that surely had never worn shoes. And as he studied these tracks, the certainty grew within him that his guesses were right. The enormous vitality of the beast-men would explain why they had not fallen before his leaden assault.

He recalled stories heard of Moros, the wild men of the Philippines, who had charged American troops and even with bullets through their hearts had survived to use bolos on their foes. They had been formidable enough enemies. But these beast-men, if he were to accept their reality, had the strength of gorillas in their hunched, powerful shoulders. They could slip silently through the underbrush, spring a dozen feet in a leap. One of their throwing stones, hurled with the full swing of a long, hairy arm, could batter a man's skull to a pulp....

"I know now what killed that policeman at the bank," Wentworth said abruptly. "A spear."

"A spear?" Conley looked dazed. "But it made a two-inch hole through his entire body—smashed two ribs...."

Wentworth said nothing. He waved the man with the lantern forward and pressed his horse close upon the other's heels.

Yes, one of those short crude spears could crash completely through a man's body. Some such fate he himself had narrowly escaped in the darkness, he knew, when he had dodged a flitting shadow. Even now those primordial killers might be creeping through the blackness of the woods, clutching stones that could brain a man, spears that could be hurled completely through a frail modern man's body....

Wentworth slipped his rifle from its scabbard and carried it across his saddle bow. He heard the soft sound of steel on leather as others followed suit. He dared not tell them what he feared, lest they flee screaming back to the security of their brick-walled homes. He steeled himself with the memory of that pitiful corpse in the woods, the woman he had been too late to save....

Overhead the wind made the trees moan. The forest tossed and threshed in a black nightmare of approaching storm. The feeble yellow gleam of the lantern made the darkness more intense. Black triangles of shadow swept wide bars across the foliage as the light passed numerous tree trunks. More than once Wentworth's hand tensed upon the stock of his rifle as he fancied he caught the gleam of eyes.

But his mount plodded on with nodding, indifferent head. The acrid odor of horse sweat was pleasant—familiar and homely amid the black uncertainty of the night.

CONLEY, BESIDE him, spoke thickly.

"We've got to hurry," he said. "There's rain on that wind, and Beth...."

"She's still alive," Wentworth answered. "Otherwise we'd have found her body."

A rasping curse tore from the sheriff's throat. "I wish we had found her body. *I wish we had!*"

They rode on, in silence save for the creak of saddle leather, the jangle of bits. There was no reply to be made to Conley. Wentworth knew what he suffered.

Many times in the Spider's battles with the Underworld, his own sweetheart, Nita van Sloan, had been seized by the criminals. They had threatened many forms of horror and death for her. But he could think of nothing, that threatened her, that would be worse than the fate in store for any woman who fell into the hands of these beast-men.

"These blood marks are getting thicker," the man with the lantern called back. "Looks like you hit him solid, all right."

Wentworth's lips moved in a twisted, hard grin. He had emptied both automatics into those creatures and already the bloody trail had led three miles into the thick hill country. The tracks lay through thick clumps of laurel now. Descents were precipitate; twice the posse had been forced to walk up steep grades. The foothills were giving way to sheer mountains, the bare tops of which lifted ruggedly against the clear night sky.

Wentworth's horse slid down a clay bank, on its haunches. Its hoofs splashed through water and then the path climbed sharply. He dropped from the saddle, hooked the rein over his shoulder, and stalked on, bent far forward, carrying his rifle in both hands. He was just behind the man with the lantern.

"I thought I saw the light glisten on that stain," he said quietly. "The blood looked fresh."

The man stopped, flashed the lantern on the blot, then stooped and ran a finger across it. When he held his hand up, a streak showed on it. The man jerked tensely and the click of his rifle's hammer as he cocked it made a loud, distinct sound in the night.

"What's up?" Sheriff Conley was quiet with an effort.

"The blood is fresh now," Wentworth told him. "The creature can't be far off."

A horse tossed its head and nickered softly. The men stood like shadows. Somewhere nearby in the bush—they could sense it—crouched the beast which had the strength to tear off a human head, which could travel three miles with a half dozen .45 caliber bullets in its body.

No one offered to advance. Wentworth himself waited, frowning. He had much more definite ideas of what was to be faced than any of the others. The man with the lantern crouched a little lower, his head pulled down between his shoulders as he took a slow step forward.

"Wait!" Wentworth ordered. He took the lantern and hooked it to his saddle, slapped the horse's rump and sent it surging forward. The horse whinnied shrilly, and shied aside from the trail Wentworth snapped his rifle up, and its blast was sharp and heavy in the close air. The horse was crashing off into the shrubbery to the right, the lantern showing spottily through the trees.

"What did you see?" Conley demanded sharply.

"A spear," Wentworth said quietly. "I need the horse to ride back."

"You shot a spear in the air!"

WENTWORTH NODDED, and pushed forward slowly, throwing a new cartridge in the chamber. "According to the throw," he added, "the beast-man is about twenty-five feet to the left of the path and fifty feet ahead. Fan out and use your pocket flashes, but wait until I've got a fifteen foot lead. I want to be close when the thing breaks cover."

Conley shoved forward. "I'm going with you."

Wentworth hesitated. He wanted a clear field of action, but he could not deny the young sheriff.

"Keep about ten feet to my right," he directed, and stepped deliberately forward. He had no way of telling whether one or two beasts crouched in the covert, nor how they were armed. Besides the spear, there could be throwing stones, knives, possibly clubs or stone-headed hammers. A single blow from any such weapon, even if it struck only a leg or arm, would probably mean destruction—unless the men behind him kept up a concentrated fire until the beast fell.

"Don't shoot unless you have to save yourself," Wentworth

With a roaring scream, one of the giants rushed straight at Wentworth!

ordered. "We're more interested in finding out where these creatures hole up than in slaughtering a few."

Sheriff Conley supported the order and they pushed on, to a
spot Wentworth calculated as being within fifteen feet of where
the beast lurked.

He halted, and dropped to one knee, the rifle thrust before
him. With his left hand he drew out his flashlight, switched it
on, and tossed it through the air toward the spot from which the
spear had been thrown. Its beam flashed in wild, spinning circles.

A screaming roar met the fall of the light and with a thunderous crashing of underbrush, a stoop-shouldered giant charged
directly toward him!

He began shooting, pumping lead at the beast as fast as his
hands could manipulate the rifle. From his right, and behind,
other rifles blasted.

Screaming, thrashing about with a mighty swinging weapon,
the beast shoved violently forward. The face was hideous. Mobile
lips snarled back from bestial yellow teeth; red, furious eyes
glared from beneath beetling brows. The thing might have been
a gorilla, but the face was too human for that.

A frenzied roar burst from the creature's mouth. With fierce
fingers it ripped at the wounds in its chest. But still it pushed
on—in the face of steady rifle fire doggedly lumbered forward.
Behind Wentworth a man cried out hoarsely and crashed off
through the underbrush in panic.

On and on came the beast, seemingly impervious to any
amount of pelting lead. Ten feet—eight feet—five… and then
it wavered, jerked up its right hand.

With a start, Wentworth saw that what the beast-man grasped was a twenty-pound sledge. It was being swung in one hand as easily as a paper-weight.

Lead still hammered into the thing's chest, bloody foam drooled from its mouth. The sledge started downward and Wentworth knew that the rifle fire would not check *that* blow.

He jerked the gun high and smashed a bullet through the beast-man's wrist. The hammer flew wide. Behind him a man screamed in terror. A sudden thud cut the scream off short. Deliberately he fired again, full into the face of the thing.

THE BEAST-MAN'S head wrenched back between his shoulder blades. From bloody jaws poured a burst of sound half scream, half roar. Feebly the great fists lifted, beat upon the chest. Then, stiffly, as a tree falls, it flopped forward on its face. It did not move again.

For a full half minute after the thing had fallen, Wentworth knelt, motionless. Except for the fact that the beast had twisted a little to the left, its head would have struck his rifle as it plunged, headlong. Slowly he got to his feet, methodically stuffed bullets into his empty magazine, levered a cartridge into the chamber. Not until then did he stoop over the motionless body and jerk it over on its back.

The face was bestial in the extreme. Chinless, with protruding yellow teeth exposed by snarling lips, small glazed eyes almost hidden in masses of hair beneath heavily ridged brows, the thing's heavy head hunched down between massively muscled shoulders, slanted forward more like an ape's than a human being's.

Wentworth's last bullet had ploughed through the skull. The chest was literally riddled with lead.

"What is it?" Sheriff Conley asked hoarsely. "In heaven's name, what is it?"

Wentworth did not answer at once. He was dazed by this graphic confirmation of his half-skeptical deductions. Then: *"Homo neanderthalensis,"* he said dully. "One of a race of primitive men supposed to have been wiped off the face of the earth by the Cro-Magnons some twenty thousand years ago."

"But the damned thing was alive!" Conley said sharply.

Wentworth's lips twisted in a wry smile. "Quite alive," he agreed. He looked about, at the clustered men staring down at the beast in the gleam of flashlights. Their faces were twisted with fear, doubt, obscure terror. They kept looking over their shoulders into the fuliginous gloom of the night. The rustle of each stirring eddy of breeze made them start.

"One of you is missing," Wentworth said. "Did that hammer...."

"The hammer killed Judson," one of the men rasped. "It smashed his skull like a melon."

At length they pushed on again, seeking, through the wind-tossed woods, some further trace of the men aeons old in the history of the race. They found no sign of others, no sign of Beth Welver. Wentworth's horse carried the body of the dead beast-man, another bore the body of the slain villager. There was an awful unreality about the entire scene, the slow trek, with that ancient beast-burden, through modern hills.

How could men of that prehistoric savage race have survived

to the present day *in these mountains?* Wentworth shook his head. He knew they had not. He recalled having read somewhere of the discovery of some primitive men in the early nineteenth century, when Tasmania had been discovered by the Dutch. They had been Cro-Magnon men who, isolated on their island, had remained in a condition akin to that of an era twelve thousand years before the dawn of civilization. Perhaps these Neanderthal men, too, had been found in some such fastness....

With tightening lips Wentworth recalled his previous certainty that human intelligence was behind the activities of these beast-men. None of them, regardless of their huge brain—actually larger than modern man's—would be capable of halting the Dixie Limited, nor would have reason for looting the Horton bank.

And if a human agency *were* behind them, it was easily possible that that agency had brought them here from some spot where they had been existing, isolated and undeveloped from ageless aeons before. Neanderthal man had ranged Europe with few, slow advancements for a hundred thousand years—for more centuries than our modern civilization has lived. It was not fantastic to assume that, isolated and under unfavorable conditions, such men might have survived with little change for a few centuries more....

THE SLOW cavalcade topped a high barren ridge and Wentworth stared out into darkness which shrouded a jumble of steep valleys and hills. The hovering clouds seemed just above their heads, and here, on the hilltop, the sweep of wind tugged and whipped at loose ends of clothing. Horses stood with their

heads drooping. The first spitting drops
of rain swept down along the avenue of
the wind.

"A light!" Conley barked sharply.
"There's a light over there."

Wentworth stared in the direction
indicated and made out a bright point
in the blackness.

"That'll be a cabin," Conley said
heavily. "We can push on there, start
out again in the morning. We couldn't
find or follow a trail in the storm coming up."

When, finally, they pulled up their weary horses before the
cabin, the rain was hammering down through the trees. The door
of the hut was flung open the next instant and a wide-shouldered man stepped upon the threshold. His shadow bulked,
enormous, before the yellow lamp light.

"Come in," he yelled into the night. "Damned glad someone
showed up after what I saw tonight...."

Wentworth strode forward swiftly.

"I took a girl away from the damndest man you ever
saw...." The man in the doorway went on.

Conley let out an excited cry and hurled forward. "A girl?
Who is she? Where...."

The man swung aside just as the sheriff charged toward the
door and then Wentworth heard Conley cry again, in great,
incredulous joy. No need to ask if he had found Beth Welver.

Wentworth stood aside while the other men trooped in.

Entering last, he faced the cabin's owner. He noted that the man was deeply tanned. A strong jaw ended in a wiry red beard. He had blue, fine eyes, which were laughing now.

"Looks like they know each other." He nodded toward his bunk. Conley was on his knees, with the girl tight in his arms. Her face, the blonde hair streaming around it, was white and wet with tears. Her eyes were closed.

"By the way," said the cabin's owner, "my name is Masters. Ted Masters."

Wentworth introduced himself. He clasped Master's firm hand then, and the two of them stepped outside. They stood under the eaves, momentarily watching the rain as it pelted down.

Finally Wentworth said: "Those 'damndest men,' as you call them, stopped the Dixie Limited tonight and massacred every soul on it. That is," grimly, "all but myself."

He saw the other's body stiffen, the ligaments in his jaw harden beneath the red beard.

"Damn!" Masters seemed to explode the word. "Excuse me, but you say that so calmly. Massacred?"

Wentworth nodded grimly. "The word is well chosen. I think I'm the only person who escaped alive—and that I did only because I tried to rescue a kidnapped woman and then fought two of the ambushers." He paused, frowning. "I give you my word—I put at least six bullets into each of them, yet one got away and the other, overtaken six miles from the spot, still had vitality enough to kill one of our party before our combined rifle-fire could bring him down."

MASTERS CURSED again, in a low hard voice. "I was luckier than I realized," he said, his voice shaken. "I went down to the spring to get some water before the storm and flashed my light at noises. I saw a half dozen of those creatures and I opened fire. One of them dropped the girl and I carried her up to my cabin. She was… pretty hysterical."

Masters was a strong broad figure in the light from his cabin. His shoulders were a little hunched. There was pugnacity in the forward thrust of his head. He blew out a deep breath.

"They gave me rather a turn," he repeated quietly, "and I'm rather used to things like that. I've been about a bit. With Jack Hawks."

Wentworth nodded. "I knew I'd heard your name. You've been after wild animals with Hawks—'Bring-'em-Back-Alive' Hawks, I believe they call him."

"That's it," Masters conceded. "And did I catch your name right? Wentworth? Richard Wentworth?"

Wentworth nodded, looked curious.

"Oh come now, you can't take that surprised attitude." Masters grinned. "No man goes through the Transvaal without hearing about that little affair with the bull elephant."

Wentworth grinned back slightly. "A bit of luck, that I managed to get in one shot and it happened to be enough."

"And happened to save the grand high muck-amuck of the Swali-hakus, or whatever they call themselves," Masters put in. "But it wasn't only that. The bull flopped down within six feet of you and you stood there looking at him, then turned around and handed your gun to the bearer and walked away lighting a cigarette. They've made a song about Wintworthi B'wana."

"Just showmanship," Wentworth laughed. "I wanted to impress the safari. They hadn't been holding up their end."

Masters let it drop, and they went inside, where Wentworth presently threw himself down on the cabin floor, for a much needed nap. They had accomplished the rescue of the girl; and morning would be time enough to pick up the trail of the beast-man—if any part of it were left after the rain.

He knew now that he had to hurry back to Paducah and fly eastward, to battle the Headsman. Now that he had confirmed his half-mad guesses on the identity of these beast-men, Sheriff Conley and his men could hunt them down as well as the Spider. But the evil brain behind their depredations... *that* was the Spider's work!

IN THE morning, with Beth Welver, Wentworth rode back to the city, leaving Masters and Sheriff Conley and the others to follow the trail.

"A plane is obviously the best method," he told Conley. "I'll send one out to help you."

Beth Welver was obviously subdued as they wound their way through the rain-drenched trees. And the fact that they carried two bodies on pack-horses did not help. She shuddered every time her eyes encountered the hairy, powerful body of the beast killed a few hours before. Her face remained pale, and purple smudges lay beneath her eyes.

With the rising of the sun, however, white mists writhed up

from the valleys and disappeared, and her spirits seemed to rise a little.

"I seem to have been lucky," she told Wentworth. "I escaped with a few bruises and scratches—and the loss of my clothes." She indicated her present costume: trousers which overlapped about her waist, and the bulging folds of a gray flannel shirt, both borrowed from Masters.

"Mister Masters—" she came out with the name primly, blushing a little beneath the delicate golden tints of her skin—"Mister Masters clothed me before I came to from my faint."

Wentworth could not help responding a little to the cheerfulness of her dimpled smile, the light of her extraordinarily blue eyes. She had not put up her hair, and its golden silk lay like a honey mist across her shoulders, whipped by the gentle breeze of her horse's movements. At the door of her home, he left her, and took the horses to the stable. Then he walked stiffly toward the hotel.

As he reached it, Jackson jumped up from a porch chair, a broad smile on his wide-jawed face. "Good hunting. Major?"

Wentworth made a wry face, dropped wearily to a chair.

"The hunting was successful, but not good," he said. "We have to deal with a band of prehistoric men—who are more powerful than gorillas, and who possess more intellect as well."

Jackson stood stiffly, unquestioning, unsurprised.

"At ease, Jackson. What's the word from New York?"

"Bad, sir. Miss Nita phoned again. This Headsman claims to have killed you. He threw a head through the window of police headquarters with a note attached, saying it was the head of the Spider… It's encouraged a lot of crooks there to act up. Robberies, murders… that sort of thing."

Wentworth's face seemed to become gaunt. His lips smiled mirthlessly. "It sounds very much like a challenge," he said thinly. "A challenge to the Spider…."

CHAPTER 4
THE CHALLENGE ANSWERED

A CHALLENGE. Yes, that was it. There could be no other reason, really, for the Headsman having pretended the murder of the Spider, Wentworth told himself. The man certainly could not be under the delusion that he actually had accomplished the Spider's death. No, it was a challenge, and it would have to be answered immediately—and terribly!

Wentworth flew back to New York that afternoon and, after a late dinner with Nita, made ready to remind the Underworld that the Spider was not dead.

He smiled quietly to himself as he lounged carelessly in the tonneau of his Lancia town car while his faithful Hindu servant, Ram Singh, wove through the after-theatre traffic. The trail he followed tonight had been set in the depths of the Kentucky hills when he had met Ted Masters, assistant and associate of "Bring-'em-Back-Alive" Jack Hawks.

He recalled that Hawks' last expedition had ended disastrously. The adventurer's ship had sunk off the Jersey coast while he was returning from a long hunting trip. There had been stories printed then of Hawks' mysterious, secret captures in little known lands far to the south, in polar waters…. A visit to Jack Hawks was in order. And if, as Wentworth anticipated, there was a connection between Hawks and the Neanderthal men in the Midwest—possibly, too, with the Headsman—there would be news of the Spider in the morning. News to drive the hopeful Underworld back into its hole!

A grim smile touched Wentworth's lips. The rising activity of criminals at news of the Spider's death was a mockery to the hopes Nita had voiced tonight. She had leaned across their table *a deux*, her white hands clasping his, her intense violet eyes gazing into his own blue ones… Wentworth's eyes closed, now, and he could almost hear the throaty music of her voice.

"Dick, you must… you *must* stop this some day," she had said softly. "It can mean nothing but your death in the end. And I have a feeling, deep inside me, that this time… this time the Spider will not win!"

She had almost gasped even in speaking such treason to the man she loved. But she had persisted, pleading with him, urging him to quit his ceaseless battling with the Underworld.

It was not that Nita herself lacked courage. Her spirit was almost too great for her frail woman's body. But she had dreams for the two of them, dreams of the day when at last the Spider might lay aside his deadly guns, might throw away forever the fearful crimson seal of the Spider and become one with the world's happy millions. The day when the Spider and his mate might build their home.

And now, suddenly, she had begun to know fear.

Wentworth jerked his head, trying to shake off the dreams. His keen glance swept through the low windows of the Lancia, at the traffic sweeping by all around him. His car was just passing the lower end of Central Park, where the golden equestrian statue sits atop its high stone base. Time to assume the disguise of the Spider.

But the dream still lingered—and Nita's warning lingered, too. It made a cold small spot in his heart as he drew down the curtains of the car windows and touched a hidden button.

The left side of the rear seat slid soundlessly forward, revolving as it moved. Nestling in its back were racks of garments. Sight of them helped him throw off the softer mood: he pulled up a mirror, illumined brilliant by hooded lights, and a shelf upon which lay the materials for every kind of facial makeup....

Ten minutes later, when the Lancia slid to a curb on a dark side street in the lower Nineties, a figure, vastly different from the dapper Wentworth, stepped from its rear.

"The usual instructions, Ram Singh." His voice came dry and hard. Then his figure merged with the darkness beside the high brick walls of the buildings.

The figure was misshapen and somehow—even barely glimpsed in the shadows—a sinister thing. From hunched shoulders swung a black long cape. The head was drawn in, poised almost venomously beneath the broad spread of a black felt. The figure leaned upon a cane.

This was the man whom all the Underworld hated and feared. This was the Spider!

The Lancia was already purring on its way. The cloaked figure did not emerge in the corner light. Somewhere in the darkness between streets, it vanished. From a dark stairway which led downward into the subterranean bowels of a high Park Avenue apartment building came the slight metallic click of a lock-pick, opening a grating. Then the door closed, and along the dimly lighted dust-heavy corridors of the furnace basement slipped the black, soundless figure.

NITA HAD often said that Wentworth talked of the Spider as if the Spider were a different person from himself.

Certainly his thoughts now lacked the cool nonchalance which was Richard Wentworth's. There was, within the Spider, a burning rage which made his eyes gleam coldly beneath the bushy black brows, thinned and straightened the lipless mouth of his disguise.

As yet he was only suspicious of Hawks. But God help the man if he were proved guilty! God help him, for the Spider wouldn't....

Up the service stairway Wentworth crept. His thoughts harked back to Nita, she had acted so strangely tonight. After that one outburst, she had made no further effort to dissuade him—but she had asked him, with a convulsive tightening in her warm, white throat, to be very careful tonight....

Wentworth fought the cold spot in his breast. It was only that Nita had had one of those strange presentiments of evil which

HEDLEY — JACK HAWKS

seize even the least superstitious of us at times. Then, too, sometimes her premonitions had been fulfilled....

Wentworth's arms crossed as he touched the bulges beneath his two arms, the two heavy automatics which nestled there. A hard grin twisted his lips.

He was at the ninth floor now. Just outside the service entrance he paused a moment, ear pressed against the door. Then he stepped into the halt, crossing to a door labeled *F.*

Deft fingers manipulated a slender lock-pick of surgical steel and seconds later he sidled into the apartment and shut the door soundlessly behind him.

The Spider did not pause in the kitchen, where he had entered, but with deliberate stealth moved across it, through a narrow butler's pantry, and a swing-door. Lights from the street filtered in dimly, the purr of Park Avenue traffic came through open windows. A curtain swayed gently in the warm breeze.

Across two more rooms, skillfully avoiding massive furniture, he drifted. He listened at three different doors against the

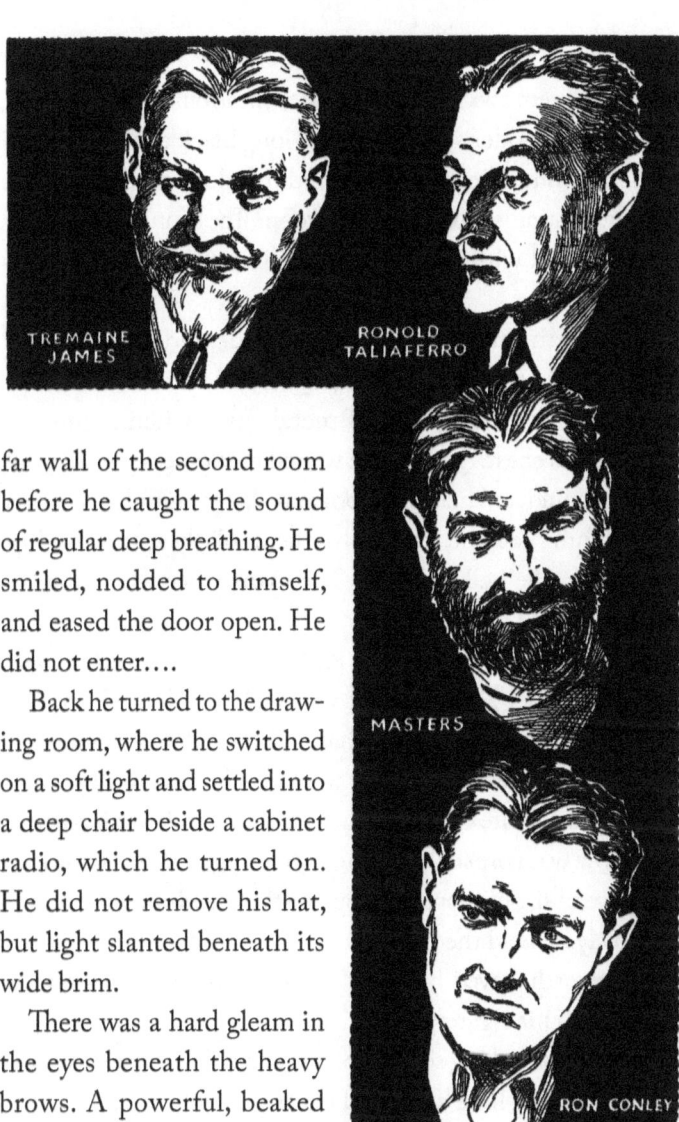

TREMAINE
JAMES

RONOLD
TALIAFERRO

MASTERS

RON CONLEY

far wall of the second room before he caught the sound of regular deep breathing. He smiled, nodded to himself, and eased the door open. He did not enter....

Back he turned to the drawing room, where he switched on a soft light and settled into a deep chair beside a cabinet radio, which he turned on. He did not remove his hat, but light slanted beneath its wide brim.

There was a hard gleam in the eyes beneath the heavy brows. A powerful, beaked nose matched well with the lipless, straight mouth. The thrust of his twisted shoulders made the Spider seem awkward as he waited, motionless, legs crossed, his left hand hidden in a fold of the long black cape.

The AC hum died out of the radio and a dance orchestra's languorous strains filtered into the room. The sound grew louder, began to thud with a heavy percussion emphasis on the bass notes.

Wentworth cut the volume down a little, and turned toward the door he had opened—the door behind which a man slept. He caught the first gleam of metal there when a gun was leveled at his chest. And still he waited motionless—until a tall, narrow-shouldered man, barefoot and clad in rumpled pajamas, stepped into the light, the revolver held solidly against his hip.

"Who in the hell are you?" The man's voice was harsh but without fright.

WENTWORTH REGARDED the other attentively. From newspaper pictures he recognized him as Jack Hawks. He was almost totally bald, and what hair he had was sunburnt to a colorless dun. Face and head were deeply browned by tropic suns, and the white of his body where the V neck of his pajamas struck low was corpselike by contrast. His gaunt length did not look powerful, but there was a suggestion of whipcord strength in the way he held the gun.

Wentworth waved his right hand lightly, fanning away the smoke from his cigarette.

"Thanks for waking so promptly," he said. His voice was debonair. "Won't you have a seat? I'd like a chat with you."

Hawks stood motionless a moment. Then something like a bleak smile touched his lips.

"You're the most unusual rascal it's ever been my pleasure to meet," he said. He circled a large soft divan without letting his revolver waver and stood in front of Wentworth about a dozen feet away, his bony feet separated a little, his body canted slightly forward.

Deliberately Wentworth scrutinized the face; the well-formed but harshly bridged nose, the taut, narrowed eyes, the lips with their hint of a bleak smile. Strength there, plenty of it. And a stark will.

"Would you mind telling me why you allowed me to walk in on you with a drawn gun?" Hawks asked. "My door was open, though I closed it when I went to bed. You could easily...."

"I wanted to talk with you," Wentworth said coolly, "and men who have slept in the jungle have a way of resenting a rude interruption to their slumbers. You might have waked up shooting."

Hawks acknowledged that with a grim nod.

"Music, they say," Wentworth smiled, "hath charms to soothe the savage beast."

His inspection of Hawks was leaving him puzzled. He knew this man had the strength to contrive the raids of the Neanderthal men. Hawks had penetrated to strange lands; he might well have discovered a primeval remnant such as these Neanderthalers obviously were. Carefully Wentworth scrubbed out his cigarette upon a tray at his side, apparently not watching Hawks.

"Neanderthal men," he began quietly—and noticed the almost suppressed jerk of Hawks' muscles. "Neanderthal men also must have had that faculty of coming awake fighting. It's contact with the crudities of nature which develops it."

Hawks spoke sharply. "Who are you and why are you here?"

"As I told you—I wanted to talk."

Wentworth was quite positive that mention of the Neanderthal men had startled Hawks. But still, the lighting was dim: he might have been mistaken. He heard the soft slap-slap of feet in the kitchen and the swing-door opened a crack, a Filipino boy slid out.

"You want something, master?"

Hawks said, "Stay there and I'll see. Well, stranger, it's your deal. Talk fast or I'll have my boy call the police! I must confess, I don't like your appearance."

Wentworth nodded. "Very well, I'll get down to business. I'm a representative of Fells-Shoto circus. We're very curious to know just what the strange animals were that you had aboard your ship last trip, and whether you can get any more."

HAWKS LOOKED at him coldly. "You're a liar," he said.

Wentworth watched—he might have been mistaken but he strongly suspected the man's finger was pressing more tightly on the trigger.

Yes, he was right! That hammer had moved backward fractionally.

And suddenly he was satisfied. This man *did* have guilty knowledge of the Neanderthal men. Even as he studied him now, Wentworth saw that there were sharp lines about the other's mouth, that the eyes seemed more sunken, and darker.

"How did you get the Neanderthal men off the ship and out

into Kentucky without their being seen, Hawks?" He asked it very casually.

Hawks came forward on light feet, which nevertheless sank deeply into the thick carpet. His gun jutted a little forward of his body now.

"Who are you?" he demanded hoarsely. "By God I'll have the truth, or...."

"Or what?" Wentworth drawled.

Hawks was only six feet away. His eyes tightened to mere slits, then widened. His mouth sagged open and he retreated three steps—quickly.

"By God," he whispered. "By God, *you're the Spider!*"

"Exactly," said Wentworth crisply. "And I might add that a forty-five automatic is in my left hand, aimed quite accurately at your solar plexus."

Hawks' still widened eyes flicked from Wentworth's face toward his left hand. He could not help but have seen the solid outline of the gun against the fold of cape.

"Order your boy to come into this room, Hawks," Wentworth ordered. "I'm more than half convinced that you turned those Neanderthal men loose on the country. If you let him call the police, I'll be wholly convinced..." He stopped, and waited.

There was no lack of courage in Hawks' dark, hard-boned face. His retreat had been an effect of surprise. His voice, when he ordered his boy into the room, was quite calm again, and stronger than it had been.

"You're supposed to be dead," he said slowly. "Your head was thrown through the window of police headquarters."

The Filipino boy, his face like brown carven wood, was standing against the far wall of the room. His small black eyes flickered from his master to the strangely cloaked man in the chair.

"Unless you talk very fast, Hawks," Wentworth said softly, "and unless you talk very convincingly, I'm afraid I shall have to leave upon your forehead concrete evidence that the Spider still lives… one of my little seals."

"If you move," Hawks said sharply, "I'll kill you."

"I won't have to move to kill you," Wentworth said slowly. "I won't even have to shoot. Don't move, for this isn't a hostile move—yet. Just a demonstration. Watch."

He cried out sharply in Hindustani and a knife flashed from the darkness, past Hawks' ear, and struck the front of the radio. Two inches of its shining steel crunched into the wood and the haft of the nine-inch knife quivered to the impact.

"So you see, Hawks," Wentworth said softly, "it would not be wise to kill me."

Hawks had not moved. But now there seemed an additional tension, a rigidity, about his body. The Filipino's mouth opened soundlessly. There was a greenish tinge on his dark face.

"Now, Hawks, will you talk?" Wentworth asked gently, "or shall I use persuasion?"

Ram Singh's harsh voice rang out from the doorway.

"*Sahib!* Behind you! Watch the door!"

CHAPTER 5
DISCOVERY OF DEATH

E VEN AS Ram Singh shouted, even while his second knife was flashing through the air, Wentworth whipped both eyes and gun toward the kitchen doorway—and caught the glint of a revolver muzzle aimed directly at him.

The Spider did two things at once. He fired with the instantaneous speed and precision for which he was famous, and he dived headforemost toward the floor. Before his dive was fairly begun, Ram Singh's knife sliced through the fabric shield of the lamp at his elbow and smashed the room into abrupt darkness.

Wentworth's single swift glance had told him that the hand holding the gun was the right, which meant that the gunman was using the door, not the wall, as a shield. His own bullet had smashed through the wood, and the following darkness was torn by a scream of mortal anguish.

Striking the floor, Wentworth rolled rapidly on the soft rug, came up on his feet, and poised tensely. His lips smiled. Besides the two nine-inch knives, Ram Singh carried an automatic which was twin to those Wentworth so expertly handled. With their combined armament and ability he and Ram Singh had stood off small armies....

In the blackness, the Filipino was squealing like a stuck pig, darting about in a frenzied effort at flight. A sharp clatter and a thud came as he tripped over a chair. He was up instantly, still yelling.

From the direction of the kitchen, a gun hammered out three

49

shots. The squealing and the blundering flight ceased immediately. There was no sound then save the Filipino's breathing, harsh and shallow. There was a rattle in his throat. It was not pleasant in the darkness, that death rattle in a dying man's throat.

But where was Hawks? No shot had come from his revolver, though he might have drilled Wentworth in that fractional instant when the Spider threw lead at the kitchen door and while Ram Singh's knife still glittered in the air. Had he been afraid of another knife in his back?

Wentworth's speculations were broken sharply as a scarcely audible whistle signaled from his right and behind him. That was Ram Singh. The Spider dropped to a crouch and echoed the sound. Seconds later, Ram Singh's hand touched his arm.

"I have my knives, *sahib*," Ram Singh whispered—and gloating lay in his voice. "Let us kill these mice who think they are men, *sahib!*"

A small smile moved Wentworth's lips. The doughty Sikh was never happier than when they fought side by side.

But with a cautioning pressure of the hand he silenced the Hindu. He had heard furtive movements to the left, beyond where the Filipino breathed his rasping last. The sound was repeated on their right. Distantly a door opened softly. No telling where Hawks was, but Wentworth was being rapidly surrounded by his enemies: that fact he knew. Also, within short minutes police would arrive, summoned by whoever had heard the shots.

Wentworth sent flat, mocking laughter into the darkness, muffling his voice with his hands so that no enemy could tell just where he was. Once more he laughed. Sinister, cold, the sounds seemed to fill the room. After them came silence—except for the harsh breathing of the Filipino.

"Fools!" Wentworth's harsh whisper stabbed through the darkness. "Fools! Would you die? The Spider kills tonight!" **GRIPPING RAM SINGH'S** arm, Wentworth crept back toward the chair he had occupied. He sat down, stationing the Hindu behind him. When police came, the criminals would fly... and the Spider had uncompleted business with Hawks.

His eyes were becoming more accustomed to the darkness now. Rays from the street shimmered faintly across the ceiling, and the furniture made black splotches. The hiss and whir of passing traffic, now and again the vicious squeal of emergency stops, floated upward to them. Then, distantly, a police radio car's siren whined.

"Now," Wentworth whispered to Ram Singh, "the mice will scamper away. Do thou, oh my brave one, follow them to their hole!"

Wentworth heard no sound, but he knew that the Hindu no longer stood behind him. He caught the vague movement of a shadow against the wall, then that, too, was gone. He himself sat motionless while the siren grew louder and was joined by three others, two of which gave off the thin, high ululation of police cars, the third being hoarser and deeper; an ambulance.

Within the house a door slammed suddenly. Feet scuttled rapidly along a hall. Wentworth smiled, nodded, and got slowly to his feet.

Circling the divan toward the door of Hawks' room, he

reached through the opening for the light switch and clicked it on. What he saw there, though, made him spring into the room, the breath hissing between his teeth.

On the floor lay a man. The gaunt, bony legs and arms were flung wide, and a dark pool had spread beneath the shoulders. It looked like Hawks, but Wentworth could not be sure. He could not be sure because—the head was gone.

A jagged curse ripped from his throat. His eyes quested sharply over the room, scanned the apartment beyond. He had been sure, when first Hawks' gun had thrust through the partly opened door, that Hawks was a party to the many crimes paralyzing the city with fear. Yet now… It seemed that a clever trap had closed upon the Spider.

But if Hawks had been killed, it put a new light on the matter. Apparently the Headsman's men had come to kill Hawks! And had succeeded despite the fact that the Spider was on the scene!

The sirens were very close now. If the Spider wished to escape… Wentworth shook his head sharply, to whip the daze from his mind. He switched off the light, sprang across the several rooms, into the kitchen, jerked open the service door….

There was a man in the hall. He had a machine gun. He crouched in the opening of the service stairway and jerked its muzzle belly-high the instant Wentworth sprang through the hallway.

Only the fact that the Spider's feet had been soundless, that he had jerked the door open with violent speed, had prevented the other from firing before Wentworth actually saw him. As it was, the Spider had a fraction of a second while that muzzle was jerking up.

Only the supremely trained reflexes of the Spider could have accomplished what he achieved in the next moment. He flung out his left hand, gripping the doorjamb as he went past. Instead of plunging straight ahead where the muzzle of the machine gun had swung to catch him, he pivoted to the left with such violence that his body, striking the wall as he circled, bounced him half across the hall.

Still reeling backward with the impetus of his movement, Wentworth snatched his guns. The machine gun was stammering, its muzzle sweeping toward him. It stitched bullet holes across the door, along the brick wall. Behind it, the killer's face was white and frightened. A man had no business dodging machine gun lead. It simply couldn't be done, even if this man in the long black cape *had* done it.

WENTWORTH'S TWO guns spoke together. Then again. Despite his crouch, the machine gunner was hammered back a pace by the Spider's lead. His weapon sagged from his bloody hands. He lifted them to his chest, where another swift stain was spreading. He was still staring with white, frightened face at the Spider.

Suddenly all expression was gone… his eyes closed, he fell back against the wall, sat down, and pitched sideways.

The Spider was breathing lightly between his teeth. His lips were drawn back, his eyes burned. This gangster had failed in his purpose of killing him, but he had succeeded even in failure.

It was too late now to escape from the apartment building. The sirens were quiet. The house would be surrounded by police.

In one stride he reached the dead gangster. Jerking the body to a seat against the wall, he pressed the base of his cigarette lighter to the man's forehead. Then he laid the machine gun across the man's knees.

It well might stay the police for a few moments to find a dead man on guard, a dead man on whose forehead was a sprawling sinister symbol the police knew and hated, a crimson blob with crooked hairy legs and poised fangs, *the seal of the Spider!*

That was Wentworth's calling card, the signature with which he had written *finis* to many a criminal career. It would surely gain him a few moments, while police stopped to curse him.

Even while he thought, he was darting again through Hawks' apartment. He found a guest chamber, rapidly stripped off his clothing. Spider cape, hat and makeup he placed on the sill of the guest room's bath, spilled over them the contents of a small vial drawn from a compact tool kit beneath his arm. Within minutes, nothing would be left of his disguise except a shapeless mess upon the window sill and a bad odor....

A chiffonier yielded pajamas. Wentworth stripped to his bronzed skin. He was a taut, handsome man. The perfect co-ordination and balance of his movements bespoke his alert mind and the hard training of his body. His muscles moved like silken snakes.

There was need for haste, and the smooth perfection of his activities wasted not a movement. Already police were sounding the door buzzer, hammering on the portals. He emptied a narcotic powder, snatched from the medicine cabinet, into a water glass. He gulped a portion of it, set the glass back on the night table, got in bed. It would take five or ten minutes for the sleeping potion to work, but the doors were stout. They would delay the police….

When police eventually found him, he was sleeping heavily and deeply. It took a doctor twenty minutes to arouse him, and then police could learn from his thick-tongued speech only that he had been visiting with Hawks, had remained overnight so that they might resume a discussion of an African trip in the morning. Sleeping potion? He had not taken any. He was very positive of that.

It was all very puzzling to the police, but of course no suspicion could attach to Richard Wentworth, scion of wealth and luxury, popular clubman, dilettante of the arts. Sympathetically, they helped him to dress, sent him to his own Fifth Avenue apartment in a taxi. He seemed quite broken up by the news that the Headsman had slain Hawks….

CHAPTER 6
NITA'S PREMONITION

THE POLICE officer sent as an escort delivered Wentworth to an impassive butler. Once the policeman had gone, Wentworth thickly ordered preparation of a drug, which swiftly dispelled the effects of the potion he had taken.

Even at this hour, Jenkyns was fully dressed, legs stiffly correct in knee breeches and hose. But his ruddy old face, beneath the smooth cap of white hair, was wrinkled with worry.

Wentworth leaned back in his chair, his brain still slightly dizzy from the reaction of the conflicting drugs.

"Ram Singh," he asked slowly. "Has he phoned?"

"No, Master Dick," Jenkyns' correctly British voice was without emotion. "Miss Nita asked that you phone as soon as you returned, sir, no matter what hour."

Wentworth nodded, waved a hand. Jenkyns brought a phone and plugged it into a socket near the chair. He knew his master would want to make this call himself.

Under the influence of the drug he had taken, Wentworth's brain was rapidly clearing. He knew that Ram Singh, sent on the trail of the Headsman's men, would call at the first possible opportunity. And when that occurred, the Spider must be ready to take the field again....

The bell had scarcely finished its first ring when Nita's voice came quietly over the wire.

"You asked that I call, *m'amie*," Wentworth said softly. Clearly he heard Nita's sigh of relief.

"I was so afraid tonight, Dick," she said. "I don't often behave this way."

Wentworth laughed. "I'm flattered, darling. You'll make me conceited, worrying about me."

"As if anyone could make you more so!" She mocked him, but her voice was gentle.

"Tomorrow afternoon—this afternoon rather—I'll call you," he promised.

Ram Singh still had not phoned when, ultimately, Wentworth fell asleep in the great soft chair beside the windows which opened on the high terrace. He did not know just when Jenkyns stole in gently, drew the shades against the graying dawn in the east, put a blanket about his knees, and tip-toed away. But he awoke at the last instant, opened his eyes, and smiled at Jenkyns' retreating back.

"Good night, Jenkyns," he called. Once more he settled himself in the chair, and slept. It was one o'clock in the afternoon when he finally had word from the Hindu. And then it was personal, for Ram Singh entered and stood rigidly, his turbaned head held high while he rebuked himself bitterly for failure. The tires had been shot off the *Lancia* by the men he pursued. He had mended the tires and returned.

THE AFTERNOON was eventful for Wentworth. Police had discovered the identity of the head tossed through the window of police headquarters and labeled as that of the Spider. The victim had been a waiter at the Ranfair Club.

Wentworth's eyes narrowed when he received that information. Captain Jack Hawks, before taking the Park Avenue apartment, had been a resident of the Ranfair club. And Wentworth was convinced that, even if Hawks were not directly responsible for the Headsman and the Neanderthal raids in Kentucky, there was some tie-up between him and the criminals. Why else would be have been slain by the Headsman?

The discovery stirred him to a new eagerness. He had been cast down by the double blow of the Headsman's victory over Hawks and Ram Singh's failure, but now he had a new clue.

He made an engagement with Nita to dine that night at the Ranfair club. The day was sweltering and even in his penthouse, sixteen stories above the street, there was no breath of wind when he prepared to leave for Nita's home.

The street was heavy with the reek of gasoline fumes. Heavy tires sucked unpleasantly at the sun-softened asphalt. The hot dusk still lingered, and men and women moved listlessly along the streets. The top decks of Fifth Avenue buses were jammed. Wentworth was listless himself until Nita was seated beside him in the *Lancia*. Then even the heat could not prevail against his pleasure in her company.

What's the business tonight, Dick?"

He smiled slowly into her violet eyes—so calm beneath the black perfection of her brows.

"I didn't say there was any business."

She laughed. But the laughter was not all gaiety. "Dick, Dick," she chided. "As if I didn't know you wouldn't take time out for a social dinner during such an affair as this."

Wentworth smiled ruefully, but made no other reply. There was none to make, of course, for Nita was right. Once the tocsin of warfare against the Underworld had sounded, Richard Wentworth took no further thought of self.

He gazed at Nita and his hand went to hers. White chiffon floated about her like foam. Her chestnut curls stirred in the warm breath of air raised by the car's passage. There was a virginal inaccessibility about Nita, sitting erectly in the corner of the seat. A little smile played sadly about her red lips.

A lump came in Wentworth's throat though his own lips

smiled. There was always bitterness amid the greatest joy that these two could know. For they loved, and yet they could not love. There could be no marriage for the Spider, upon whom the heavy hand of disgrace might fall at any time—no marriage, no home, no children.

God knew he had battled against this love. But it had proved stronger than he, stronger than their combined wills. They had made concessions to their love. While criminals continued to menace the world, the Spider might not lay down his arms. But at least they would fight against humanity's foes side by side; at least they might have the pleasure of mutual battle.

YES, THERE had been times when his heart had wavered, times when he had been torn between love and their stern pledge to ignore each other's safety and happiness if it came to a choice between themselves and humanity. But he had clung to duty....

He thrust the heavy thoughts from his mind and something like a sigh pushed out through his tight lips.

"Jackson phoned me this afternoon," he said slowly. "The planes failed to find any trace of the Neanderthal men, and the searchers on the ground had no better luck. There's been a movement started to have the governor of the state remove Sheriff Roy Conley for cowardice. That girl's father, Ben Welver, has disappeared entirely. He started out to follow us into the hills the night the girl was carried off. He never came back."

Nita patted his hand. "Are you sure, Dick, that some one is behind these Neanderthal men? Wouldn't it have been possible for them to have become isolated in the hills there...."

Her voice dwindled off. She recognized the impossibility of

her speculations, even as she talked. She sighed. "You didn't learn anything from Hawks?"

"Not a thing." He turned to her. "What's the matter, dear? You're gloomy tonight." He shook her arm gently. "Not letting those premonitions of yours still run wild, are you?"

She laughed lightly, shook her head, leaned toward him with eyes half closed, lips provocative. "But I do so love to run wild, Dick," she whispered.

Wentworth's hand tightened on her arm, his breath came a little quickly.

"You darling!"

He caught her to him, and his lips sought hers hungrily. For a long moment she lay upon his arm. Then she pushed languidly away. She was smiling, mockingly coy.

"Oh, Mister Wentworth," she cried. "I don't know what made you think I was that kind of girl. And besides… somebody might have seen us!"

Wentworth laughed, kissed her again. "Adorable!" he whispered.

When Ram Singh tooled the car up to the entrance of the Ranfair, Nita's hands were busy with her hair. The two laughed again as their eyes met. Wentworth clung desperately to their moment of gaiety as they sauntered up the broad, lighted steps of the club. It seemed to him there was always a desperate strain about their love-making. Each kiss, with death ever at his elbow, might well be their last.

The *chasseur* swung the door wide and the two strolled in. Envious eyes had turned on them from the streets. Wentworth was resplendent in full evening dress, high silk hat upon his head, cane tucked beneath his arm. Nita seemed to float along in her foaming chiffon. And both were so obviously well pleased to be in each other's company.

The headwaiter bowed obsequiously and led them to a palm-screened table *a deux*, not too far from the dance floor. He stood beaming, silver pencil poised above his card. He took their orders with delighted solicitous murmurs. Chincoteague oysters on the half-shell? Green turtle soup? If he might be so bold as to suggest—the Pomona was su-*perb!* But yes, m'sieur, *au muniere*. Breast of guinea hen? A *salade?* He himself would attend to that *salade*. There was an excellent 1912 Burgundy and the guinea hen was of a nice gaminess. Mr. Wentworth's favorite *Chablis* with the oysters?

Wentworth smiled at Nita, ordering carelessly. "Yes, dear," he said, "it's business tonight, but just what business I'm not sure." He told her what faint clues pointed to the Ranfair club as having some possible connection with the Headsman.

"I don't," he admitted, "know just what I hope to accomplish, but if your premonitions are correct, something will undoubtedly turn up."

THE *chablis* was set beside them in a silver ice bucket and the second *savarin* cocktail was half consumed when Wentworth's carelessly alert eyes caught a familiar figure across the room.

"Glastonbury," he murmured to Nita. "Our esteemed former district attorney. I haven't seen him since the day he had me up for one of the few murders that I haven't committed."

Nita watched Glastonbury's short, bobbing stride as he paced across the room, brows set in their perpetual scowl, lip corners pulled down.

"I don't suppose anything ever satisfied him in his life," she said cheerfully. "He'll probably want to revise the admittance rules of heaven."

"To keep me out?" Wentworth laughed. "Who's the chubby old duffer with him?"

The two, Glastonbury and the chubby stranger who waddled cheerfully along beside him, were very close now, being led by the suave head waiter directly past Wentworth's table. Nita barely had time to murmur "Tremaine James" when the man saw her and, smiling more widely than ever, turned deliberately toward their table.

"My dear, my dear!" he cried. "I haven't seen you in a dog's age. Do you think you treat an old man quite fairly?"

Wentworth was on his feet, smiling politely. Tremaine James was as rotund as a cupid, short, and well padded with fat. His cheeks were rosy and unwrinkled, and lips almost too red made a neat little bow between waxed white mustaches and a pointed van dyke. His well trained hair lay in a neat white mantle across a cheerful brow.

"I've simply been forgetful," Nita laughed. She waved her hand at Wentworth. "Dick, an old friend of my father's. He'll probably be bragging in a few moments that he held me on his knee. Richard Wentworth, Tremaine James."

Wentworth bowed. "I warn you I'm inordinately jealous," he said with a false scowl. "Don't say a word about this business of sitting on knees or you'll probably be challenged to a duel by morning."

Tremaine James' bright small eyes twinkled. "Come here, Glastonbury," he cried. "This man is threatening me with a duel."

Glastonbury stood on belligerently braced legs, an irate bull terrier, his bulging eyes scowling from behind horn-rimmed spectacles. He sneered.

"Wentworth has murdered men before this," he said in his clear harsh voice.

Wentworth's smile faded. Nita stiffened in her seat. A look of bewilderment crossed Tremaine James' jolly face. "I do believe, Glastonbury, that you're taking me seriously," he complained.

Glastonbury reached the table in two jerky strides.

"I see, Wentworth, that you were present in Hawks' apartment last night when he was murdered," he said sharply. "Although the Spider had made a kill there, you weren't held."

"Dick," said Nita, "I just love to waltz and...."

THE MUSIC of the orchestra swelled gently through the room. An electric fan made the fronds of the artificial palms rustle metallically as it swept air across them. Wentworth bowed, offered an arm to Nita.

"I'm sure, Mr. James, that you'll excuse us," Nita said brightly.

"I had thought," Glastonbury pounded on, leaning both hands on the table, "that with Kirkpatrick out of the police department, we would have honest administration of the law against the Spider."

At the words, Wentworth's smile vanished and tension stiffened his body. Others in the club were noticing the disturbance now. The headwaiter was fluttering in the background. Wentworth felt Nita grip his arm tightly. But he turned quietly back to the table, faced Glastonbury across its gleaming whiteness.

Kirkpatrick was Wentworth's close friend. Throughout Kirkpatrick's regime as police commissioner, the two had worked together to suppress crime. Kirkpatrick had been convinced that his friend was the Spider, but the proof had never fallen into his hands and because he thought the Spider did a noble work in defense of humanity, he had agreed to help him.

But Kirkpatrick would never have dodged his duty. If the evidence fell into his hands, he pressed it vigorously. If Wentworth were to come before him, now that Kirkpatrick was governor, and plead for pardon from the electric chair, Kirkpatrick would refuse, Wentworth knew, for Kirkpatrick never played favorites in the execution of his stern duty. That was why Wentworth's anger stirred hotly within him now at Glastonbury's words.

"Just what do you mean to imply, Glastonbury?" He demanded it quietly. He knew that he ought not bandy words with the doughty little lawyer, but the insult to Kirkpatrick....

"You know damned well what I mean," Glastonbury rasped. "I mean Kirkpatrick protected you in your operations as the Spider. I mean that without Kirkpatrick as head of the police, you would have been laid by the heels long ago."

Wentworth was hard put to fight down his anger. His eyes gleamed with cold menacing lights. "That's two libels within a minute, Glastonbury," he said coldly. "You libel the governor and you libel me. If I were you I would learn to control my tongue a little better."

Tremaine James' face was ludicrous with bewilderment. He patted Glastonbury on the arm and said ineffectually, "Now, now, Glastonbury, let's not be unreasonable."

Glastonbury's sneer grew more pronounced. Fury trembled in every inch of his vibrant small body.

"I stand behind what I say," he bellowed, his voice rising. "You are a murderer and Kirkpatrick…."

"Shut up, you two-center," Wentworth snapped. "If these things are true and you failed to prove it, you were a damned poor prosecutor!"

"I can prove them now!"

Wentworth leaned forward, patted the table with the palms of his hand.

"Shut up, Glastonbury," he said. "You are an execrable district attorney. As a lawyer you do not appeal to me. And as a gentleman, you are a total loss. If you….

RAGE OVERWHELMED Glastonbury. He caught up a glass from the table and hurled its contents into Wentworth's face. Wentworth's upflung arm barely protected his eyes.

He stood rigidly, lungs pumping with anger. Slowly, he drew a handkerchief from his pocket and dried his face.

"Thanks for your confirmation of my statement," he said in a voice utterly devoid of expression. He turned his back.

"Nita, shall we dance?"

When they returned to their table, Glastonbury was gone.

Tremaine James, his chubby, rosy-cheeked face very woebegone and apologetic, was waiting for them.

"I hope you won't hold me responsible for all this," he said abjectly. "The truth is I've had a few business dealings with Glastonbury and we were here on business tonight. I'd proposed him for club membership, but I shall, of course, immediately withdraw that. The little bounder...."

Wentworth could smile now. "It really is an affair of no moment," he said. "We were antagonists once. His defeat has probably embittered him."

When Tremaine James had gone, Wentworth stared down at the table for a long while. As he looked up, he saw that Nita's white teeth were fastened on her lip.

"What is it, dear?" she whispered.

Wentworth moved about the table to her side, put a steadying hand upon her shoulder.

"What, darling?"

"This means trouble, Dick," Nita still whispered. "This is my premonition of trouble. Glastonbury.... Glastonbury is in a murderous rage."

Wentworth laughed lightly. "Flattering me again, darling," he said. "Glastonbury has been in murderous rages before this, and with me."

Nita did not laugh. Her shoulders shuddered beneath his hand. She said, "I'm afraid."

CHAPTER 7
A ONE-SIDED DUEL

WENTWORTH WAS at a loss to explain Glaston-bury's attack upon him. There was no secret about their mutual dislike, but... He shrugged it aside. It was useless to worry about it He had come here with the definite purpose of learning something about the waiter who had been killed.

The *maitre d'hôtel* was desolated that Wentworth's usual waiter was not with them tonight. The *canaille* had left without notice two days ago. Captain Hawks, the man prattled on, had been greatly annoyed at finding a strange man attending him.

"Ah. Then Captain Hawks was accustomed to dine here. Perhaps even at this very table?" Wentworth queried.

The headwaiter indicated a table a short distance away, then, reading his dismissal, bowed himself away.

Wentworth smiled thinly. "It looks very much, my dear, as if that waiter were killed because he overheard something Hawks said. If someone had merely wished to put a spy on Hawks, it would not have been necessary to kill the other man."

Nita was distrait. The smile upon her lips was artificial and her deep violet eyes kept questing over the room.

"But Hawks has been killed by the Headsman," she protested. "And what you say indicates that Hawks and the Headsman were allies."

Wentworth nodded. "Exactly. This wouldn't be the first time a criminal had hidden himself by pretending that he had been killed by the agency with which he was connected. Hawks might well have prepared that. But how he could have known I'd be there, I don't know."

"But you saw Hawks' body!"

Wentworth's eyes grew quizzical. "Yes, darling. But the head was gone. And many bodies, without heads, look very much alike."

He went on more slowly. "On thinking the affair over, I am quite sure that the attack in Hawks' apartment was all staged for my benefit. The machine gunner's attempt to kill me was the work of an underling who did not know his master's full plans. There's no doubt in my mind that the criminals knew somehow that I was going to Hawks' apartment."

He frowned, trying to discover how they had learned his plans. It could not have been an accidental sight of his entrance, because, assuming that his theory of Hawks' falsified death was correct, it would have taken time to find a man whose appearance was similar in order to make the substitution.

Nita's folded hands were upon the table, and her fingers were white with pressure. "They are not through with you!" she cried. "That was just the first step in an attack against you!"

Wentworth reached out, covered both her white small hands with his brown one. The orchestra began another softly sensuous rhythm and presently a few couples began to circle the polished strip of floor among the palms. Wentworth patted Nita's hands. Still she leaned forward, unsmiling, her face white and drawn.

"Isn't it so, Dick?" she demanded. "Don't you know it was all part of some major attack upon you?"

"Probably," he agreed carelessly, "but that's been tried before, dear. Why concern yourself? That isn't like my brave girl."

Nita shook her head vehemently. "I'm not brave. I'm very much afraid tonight." She stood up suddenly. "Dick, I want to go home."

WENTWORTH WAS instantly on his feet. The waiter slid obsequiously forward. Nita's smile came mechanically to her lips and the two bowed graciously a dozen times to acquaintances as they went out. In the foyer a page boy, with a pillbox hat set jauntily on his head, stepped forward, clicked heels and presented a silver tray. Wentworth plucked up the white envelope, smiling at the alert, stiff-backed youngster. He laid a coin on the tray and the boy snapped to salute and marched off.

Wentworth tapped the envelope thoughtfully against the nails of his left hand. Nita's eyes, gazing up into his, were frightened.

"Quickly, Dick," she urged. Her voice was little more than a whisper. "Open it."

"Nice kid," Wentworth said absently. "His father was a policeman."

"What are you talking about?"

Wentworth said, "The page boy," and slid a crisp leaf of vellum from the envelope. He skimmed over it with a little frown, then shoved it into his pocket. Nita said nothing until they were again in the Lancia. There Wentworth put his arm lightly about her shoulders.

"The Spider has offended my very dear friend, Glastonbury," Wentworth quoted the letter, his voice flat. "I hope he will not refuse me satisfaction. The rocks in Central Park oppo-site Eighty-ninth street at dawn. I have heard it said that the Spider never refuses a challenge."

Nita's deep breath quivered in her throat. She did not speak, but her hands clung to his. Nothing, she knew, could keep Wentworth from meeting the challenge.

"It was signed 'The Headsman,'" Wentworth added dryly.

"Does that mean Glastonbury is one of the criminals?" Nita asked quickly.

Wentworth shook his head. "It's a pretext, I imagine, to make me realize I am under the Headsman's surveillance. Anyone in the club dining-room tonight could have supplied the infor-mation."

His keen eyes were puzzled as, now and again, he glanced into the small rear-vision mirror, set in the tonneau of the car. So far as he could discover, he was not being followed.

He left Nita at the door of her apartment, and for a moment she clung to him, face blindly lifted to his caress.

"Phone me soon, Dick. Soon?" she implored.

"Of course, darling." He gently pushed her inside.

The Lancia wove smoothly through the streets. In it, Went-worth sat rigidly erect, watching his backtrail without seeming to do so.

This Headsman was a most elusive foe. The evidences of his existence were everywhere, but the man himself remained as nebulous as invisible gas.

His mind reverted again to his certainty that his arrival in

Hawks' home had been expected. And then he jerked upright, as a new thought struck him.

He had visited Hawks *because Ted Masters had mentioned him.*

Did that mean, then, that Masters had deliberately mentioned Hawks to recall the fact that his ship had been sunk? Did that mean that Masters was party to the crimes? Wentworth's eyes became dreamily speculative. Jackson, whom he had left in Kentucky, could investigate that possibility.

Impatiently Wentworth shook his head. That would presuppose that Masters knew Wentworth to be the Spider, which was impossible. Probably the Headsman had counted on the newspaper stories about Hawks' "strange discovery" to lead the Spider to his home. There had been an item the day before, an interview with Hawks on head hunters....

THE HEAT of the July day was fading, the warmth leaking from pavement and stone walls. A little vagrant breeze fought the gasoline fumes. In Wentworth's penthouse, the curtains performed a solemn, slow dance.

Ram Singh bought an extra of the morning papers and Wentworth read black headlines which screamed of horror.

A transcontinental bus had been found at the roadside, its passengers horribly dead or vanished—the work of some of the Neanderthal horde. Kentucky was mobilizing its militia. In San Francisco, four officers of a leading gold mine company had been murdered all in one night. In each case the body had been ripped open with a knife and the heart torn out.

An eminent scientist, linking the San Francisco crimes, the Headsman murders, and the forays of the Neanderthal men, as indicating a new barbaric middle ages, spoke learnedly of a return to heliolithic culture.

Wentworth read the papers with feverish eyes, jaws locked in anger. While he grappled blindly with a killer in New York, murder stalked the nation. And still there seemed to be no motive behind the senseless massacres. None at least that met the eye.

Frowningly he began to itemize his knowledge of the events which had led up to the Headsman's challenge. He had not told Nita, but he was confident now that the trap in the Hawks' apartment had been for the purpose of identifying the real personality behind the Spider. That had been accomplished either through trailing Ram Singh, or through the knowledge of the crooks that Wentworth had not been a house guest of Hawks.

The entire situation was damnably irritating. The Spider could battle the killers of the master criminal who, he felt sure, was behind all these murderous outbreaks. He could go west and tramp the hills of Kentucky in the wake of the Neanderthal men. But these were all side issues—tasks which could be performed equally well by police or militia. The leader, the leader himself was the man to get at. And of him there was no trace. Wentworth sprang to his feet and began to pace restlessly across the room.

So far, he was positive he had not met the leader of these hordes. Hawks, if indeed he were still alive, well might be the motivating force behind the Neanderthal men. But the Headsman killings? He did not know. Of course, the various crimes might be the work of as many different groups of criminals. It was certain that these "heliolithic" killings in San Francisco and the Headsman murders in New York were planned and had a purpose.

It was notable that, with the exception of Hawks and the Ranfair waiter, all the New York victims had been men of industrial prominence. The four who had died in San Francisco had all been prominent in gold mining. Some capitalists might have turned to crime....

Only the raids of the Neanderthal men seemed purposeless, and Wentworth could not convince himself that primitive men had been transported across oceans and loosed in the Middle West without some greater purpose than merely allowing them to plunder and kill.

With long deliberate strides, Wentworth entered, through a dark high arch, his music room. From a stand beside the serrated points of the organ pipes he caught up his violin and, with it tenderly in his hands, walked out upon the terrace beneath the night skies. Here, sixteen stories above the street, the stars were clearer, though the haze of city lights built a curtain against the sky.

Tucking the violin beneath his chin he gently tuned the strings. A moment's pause, a moment of deep, utter silence, and he began to stroke wild music from the instrument, wild sound that went soaring toward the stars. He had a marvelous skill, an uncanny feeling for the instrument. Much that he played was extemporaneous composition, and through it he calmed his mind and soul.

TIME PASSED without consideration. But in going inside finally, he realized with a start that his dawn duel with the Headsman was less than an hour away. The heat had evaporated and the cool breath of the pre-dawn night drifted in through the open windows. He felt an immense weariness, a sharp reluctance which brought a tight frown to his forehead. When had the Spider ever shirked a battle with his enemies? When had he regretted a challenge?

He thrust his reluctance aside and called Ram Singh. Then, with the Hindu driving once more, he started in the Lancia for the designated meeting place with the Headsman. A great driving eagerness lay in him now, a hope that at last he would meet with the leader of this great conspiracy spreading terror and death over the nation. And—once more he wore the garb of the Spider. His hunched shoulders, his beaked face below the wide brim of his hat, carried menace.

The car skimmed quietly up Fifth Avenue, to a point where he spotted the bald crown of rock which rose above the level of the park trees at Eighty-ninth street. It was a familiar spot to him but beholding it again in the faint gray light of false dawn, he frowned. It was a ridiculous spot for a duel, within plain view—or rifle shot—of half a dozen high apartment buildings. He was suddenly sure that this challenge was a trick to snare the Spider. Yet he could not evade the challenge.

A fleeting memory of Nita's fears came to him and he shook his head angrily. Premonition? He moved always in the midst of danger. As for this being a trap, there could be no doubt of that. Criminals except in rare cases, did not for a moment consider fair play in contesting with the Spider. They decided on his death and took the most direct, the surest method of accomplishing that. Wentworth hoped savagely that the Headsman himself would be present. He was weary with hammering at straw walls which hid nothing of importance....

"Take the Eighty-sixth street crosscut," he ordered sharply. The Lancia swung right at the next corner, drifted south on Madison, then sped west again through the walled cross-cut which burrowed beneath the park. At a point where thick trees hung out above the cut, the Lancia checked a moment, then muttered on. In that instant, a shadow had overleaped the wall.

The Spider was approaching his rendezvous.

Under the trees, the faint gray light had not yet penetrated. Wentworth moved there with absolute silence, the consummate skill which his many seasons in the forests had given him. The bare crown of rock on which he was to meet the Headsman was three hundred yards to the north. He moved toward it deliberately, ears and eyes attuned to the world of shadows through which he advanced.

He was a hundred yards away from the place when he merged his body with the thick blackness under a shrub and crouched motionless, breathing through his open mouth. Fine hard lines stood in the corners of his eyes. He had caught a whisper of movement not five yards ahead where the shrubbery, beside which he poised, merged into a dense thicket. Movement. The Spider's keen ears assured him of that. But as yet he could see nothing at all.

Nevertheless he could not delay. Presently the rising sun

would strike across the tops of the trees. And the sight of the Spider meant his death, whether blue-coated police or lurking gangster first spotted his hunched, black-cloaked figure.

A faint smile touched Wentworth's lips. He straightened from his covert and strolled openly forward, humming a light tune beneath his breath.

HE KEPT his eyes focused on the spot from which the sound had come, and he heard new movement as he advanced. It was very close now. In moments he would be beside the hiding place. Steadily he walked on, with a cool nonchalance which mocked the triphammer beating of his heart.

He was almost upon the place. He cuddled a blackjack in his right palm, and in his left a miniature flashlight. He was ready.

Another stride. Another....

Now!

From the flashlight held low against his side, Wentworth spilled radiance into the thicket. A man started erect, with gun leveled, and the light glittered on brass buttons. The brass burtons and shield of a policeman!

So this was the trap of the Headsman! He had summoned the Spider to the spot and surrounded it with police. Knowing that the Spider did not battle police, would never loose his guns against them, he had deliberately plotted his enemy's extinction!

Wentworth was secure for the moment in the knowledge that the policeman could not see the person behind the blinding light. He coarsened his voice, affected a vulgar accent.

"Geez! A cop!" he gasped. "What are youse...."

"Douse that light!" the policeman rasped.

Wentworth saw that the officer, too, held a flashlight. If he turned it on, he would see the Spider, recognize him….

This was the moment, or never! With a gulped murmur of simulated fright, Wentworth cut off his light and in the same instant, leaped forward with the blackjack. Long practice had made his movements as sure in the darkness as in broad day. His leap was soundless and the blackjack swung true. He caught the policeman's body as it went limp, and lowered it gently to earth. The officer's flashlight and gun had already thudded down.

Wentworth jerked erect as he heard further movement nearby. He crouched rigidly.

"What's going on over there, Jim?" a cautious voice called. Wentworth muffled his mouth with his hand. "A bum," he whispered back. "The dumb egg got scared and I had to slug him."

A grunt answered him and he waited, unmoving, scarcely breathing, to see if the other officer would investigate. His heart seemed beating in his very throat, hard and heavily. The white scar along his right temple, scar of a knife fight long ago, throbbed.

Small restless sounds come from where the other man had called. If he were to come this way…. But presently the sounds ceased and Wentworth nodded in the darkness. He was safe for the moment. His hand touched his victim's pulse and he nodded again. The man would be out for a good half hour.

There was a tight, thin smile on Wentworth's lips as he pushed deliberately on toward the stone crown. Foolhardy, it might be, to enter what he knew to be a hidden cordon of police. But the Headsman must know that the Spider had kept his engagement.

Without meeting further obstacles, he reached the last fringe of bushes. From here to the top of the rocks was no more than fifty feet. Yet it was the most dangerous stretch of all. The false dawn, the reflected light of the rising sun against the sky, had faded and there was an inky darkness, but it would last for moments only....

WENTWORTH THRUST the base of the large hand torch he had taken from the policeman into the earth and laid a folded handkerchief over its lens. He attached the end of a long light length of silken cord—the sort he always carried: powerful stuff less than the diameter of a pencil—to the light, then crawled five yards to the left and thrust the policeman's pistol under a rock, securing its trigger to the other end of the cord.

He was ready now, ready to mount the crest and sound his challenge to the Headsman, treacherous killer that he was.

Slowly he inched toward the crown of rock. Only ten feet to go now, ten feet. But if he advanced even half of that, he would be outlined against the sky—a hunched, be-cloaked figure no policeman could mistake. His first appearance would be the signal for a hail of lead nothing could have survived.

Deliberately, he jiggled the silken cord. It shook the pad of cloth from over the flashlight lens and a beam of light cut straight up into the blackness of the night. He yanked the other part of the cord and the revolver blasted under the rock where had wedged it; blasted once, twice, a third time. He tugged at the flashlight and it flopped over flat on the ground.

Against its beam, he saw a man running toward the spot. Pandemonium broke out on all sides. Policemen shouted and called excitedly back and forth. Wentworth fired the hidden pistol twice more, then crawled to the crest of the rock and placed there the challenge from the Headsman on which was printed the red seal of the Spider.

It took only an instant, then he was creeping down from the rocky ridge on the opposite side. The crashing in the underbrush was tumultuous. At least twenty men were rushing about there. He straightened, started running wildly in the shrubbery.

"The Spider!" he shouted. "The Spider. He's over there, by the light."

He fired twice straight up into the air. His cry stirred added excitement. Flashlight beams flicked everywhere. For a moment longer, he crashed about in the shrubbery, then made use again of his woodcraft and drifted silently away.

The shouts faded with distance. He turned inward toward the park drive. At a curve in the road, a low-swung, powerful automobile hesitated a moment, then purred on. It was stopped at the northern exit, but police had no reason for holding the suave gentleman within—who obviously was returning very late from a very gay party. The gentleman still had a flask half full in his pocket. It was very good whiskey, the policeman agreed.

CHAPTER 8
TEETH OF THE TRAP

SHERIFF RON CONLEY arose from the divan as Wentworth walked into the drawing-room of his penthouse and stalked forward with an outstretched hand.

"I'm hoping you'll pardon me for breaking in on you like this," Conley said in his grave young voice. "Fact is, they kind of kicked me out and I thought...."

Wentworth gestured courteously. "Sit down, Sheriff." He handed his hat and cane to Jenkyns, ordered drinks and seated himself beside Conley.

He was puzzled. Why had this man left Kentucky to follow him?

"What can I do for you, Sheriff?" His face showed only polite interest.

A quick boyish smile crossed Conley's face, showing the even white rows of his teeth. "I'm not sheriff any more," he said ruefully. "They suspended me on charges of cowardice." The smile faded and left his face strangely grim. "I lost my temper and resigned. It was foolish, but it was damned hard to have folks I grew up with thinking I'd lie down on my job and let those... those *things* run off with Beth."

Wentworth offered one of his specially blended cigarettes, lighted one himself and leaned back, studying the other. He waited.

"I'm convinced," Conley said finally, "that the same folks that got me out of a job are behind those Nean—Neander... whatever they are, sir. I was talking about it with your man, Jackson, and he advised me to come here and see you. Masters thought it would be a good idea, too, so I did it. We want you to come and help us find out who-all is behind this business. It's pretty terrible out in Kentucky, sir." He drew a long breath; went on.

"At night the houses are locked up tight, the blinds shut, the men sleeping with their guns loaded and cocked. And to think there's men who could turn loose beasts like that, on human beings…."

Presently he explained how he and others had arrived at the conclusion that there was someone behind the raids of the Neanderthal man. The reasoning corresponded with Wentworth's own.

"It was Master's idea first," the visitor added. "We think you could do a wonderful lot of good out there, sir. Masters was telling us about what you did in Africa. And I remember reading how you helped run down some pretty big criminals here in America, sir. Would you… would you come out to Kentucky and help us?"

Wentworth rubbed out his cigarette in an ashtray carved from an elephant's tusk. He closed his eyes.

He was heavy with fatigue. The night which had promised so well was past without achievement. Dawn spilled an ugly grayish light across the floor. The sky was paling to blue and there was renewed promise of unrelenting heat for the day.

Even his mind seemed to move sluggishly. He had thought Masters responsible for the affair at Hawks' apartment. Now it appeared Masters was working with him, wanted his help in Kentucky.

"Who was behind your suspension?" he asked.

"Welver's step-brother," Conley replied shortly. "Calls himself Taliaferro. He came to Kentucky from Nevada just to get me out."

WENTWORTH'S EYES opened. "Nevada? Taliaferro isn't by any chance interested in gold mines?"

Conley's eyes widened. "How did you know?"

Wentworth shook his head. Gold mines. Was there a tie-up between the California murders and Taliaferro?

Jenkyns brought in a tray and set it on a low table of inlaid teak before the divan. Presently Wentworth stirred himself to offer his visitor a glass of Scotch and soda, and take one for himself. Its cool dry flavor was pleasant on his palate.

"I'll have to think it over, Conley," he said slowly. "You've heard of the Headsman crimes here in the city, I imagine. I've been working on those...."

A distant dry whirring stopped his words and he turned his heavy eyes toward the arched entrance of the room.

"We seem to be having other late callers, Conley," he said.

Jenkyns' dignified form moved across the archway, to return presently as far as the doorway, from where he announced:

"Commissioner Flynn."

Wentworth strolled toward the door with a puzzled frown as the gaunt tall police commissioner strode jerkily into the room.

Even in his civilian clothes, Flynn would have been picked anywhere for a soldier. His white hair sat like a military cap on his forehead and his lean, thin-nosed face had the grim set of a man used to command... as well as obedience. He was at least three inches over six feet, but his movements were as alert and sharp as those of a lightweight.

"Glad you're awake," Flynn chopped out the words. "Bad time to call, but it's important."

82

Wentworth said, "Always glad to see you, Commissioner. This is Ron Conley, until recently sheriff in Hobart, Kentucky."

Flynn's sharp blue eyes bored into Conley. The introduction was acknowledged with a brief nod.

"Damned unpleasant business, Wentworth." Flynn hesitated. "Where have you been tonight?"

Wentworth lifted his brows. "I'm glad it's you who asked, Commissioner," he said slowly. "From anyone else, I'd have to request an explanation, and even then, I might consider the question impudent."

He lifted his shoulders slightly, gestured Flynn to a seat in a large easy chair facing the divan. "Do you like ice, Commissioner?"

"None, thanks." Flynn sank into the chair, but did not relax. He sat there bolt upright, his head rigidly erect on his neck, frowning. His piercing blue eyes never left Wentworth. But they looked a little relieved now.

When Wentworth had given him the drink and seated himself, he smiled wintrily.

"Know this is imposition. This time of night," he said. "But had to see you."

"Quite all right," Wentworth assured him. "Now, you wanted to know what I did tonight?"

Flynn nodded. "Please."

Wentworth detailed the dinner at the Ranfair, his return home, and the music on the terrace.

"I was restless," he went on. "Crimes such as this Headsman has committed infuriate me. I went for a drive in the park and had just returned home a few moments ago to find Mr. Conley here. He wants me to help them fight the Neanderthal men in Kentucky."

Flynn's face seemed to acquire more sharply chiseled lines. "When did you leave the house?"

"I'm not quite sure," Wentworth told him. He kept idly sipping his drink. "About three o'clock, I imagine."

Flynn looked down at the amber mixture in his glass.

"Glastonbury was murdered at three-thirty," he said slowly. "Home on Park Avenue, east nineties."

His eyes lifted quickly, took in the blank surprise of Wentworth's face. "Your quarrel at Ranfair. Elevator boy at Glastonbury place described visitor. Fits you. Found this…" He held out a surprisingly well shaped hand, well cared for except for tobacco stains on two fingers. On his palm glittered a broken cuff-link. "Your initial," he said.

Wentworth leaned forward slowly, stiffly, a frown making a vertical slot between his eyes. His brain was whirling.

Glastonbury murdered! The doughty little man with whom he had quarreled at the Ranfair, slain at his home at precisely the time set for the Spider to face the Headsman on the rocky eminence in the park. The Headsman had made carefully sure that Wentworth would not have a usable alibi, then had planted evidence to connect him with the crime!

EVEN IN the first shock of surprise Wentworth had no doubt of the identity of the man who was framing him. It was the Headsman. Wentworth's every movement since his return to

New York had been ordered by the Headsman to this ultimate goal—a frame-up for murder.

"It *is* my cuff-link," he said. His voice sounded strange and hard, even to his own ears. "But it just so happens that I haven't worn that set of links in weeks."

He swallowed slowly, leaned back, and stared at his own drink. He fought down the sudden fierce anger which stirred within him—an anger actually mixed with slight admiration. The Headsman had planned well. First a trap rigged to identify him, then a public pretense for a quarrel, finally a challenge to make sure there would be no alibi… Oh, yes, the Headsman had planned well, damnably so. A worthy adversary for the Spider.

He cleared his throat, twice, in fact, before words came.

"I don't know what I can say, Commissioner." He smiled a little, lifted his eyes to meet the keen blue gaze of Flynn. "The only thing I could do would be cry frame-up, which is the truth, but a very poor defense. I can give you my solemn word…."

He shrugged, cut off the phrase. "Do you want me to go to headquarters with you? I appreciate your coming personally."

It was a struggle to make his words, his voice calm.

Ron Conley seemed stunned. He sat staring first at one man, then the other. There was anger in the thinning of his lips.

"Great deal you could say," Flynn said gruffly. "First place, too much sense to murder at such a time of day. Foolishness. Too easy to trace anyone. Another thing. Entrance by elevator and easy identification. Foolishness. One thing looks like you. Glastonbury apparently killed in a duel. Pistols at less than ten paces. You'd do that sort of thing."

Wentworth's smile made his lips ironical. "Yes, I would," he agreed quietly.

The Headsman had indeed planned well!

"Also, Glastonbury gave me every provocation, even the traditional one of throwing a drink into my face. It's clever, damnably clever, Flynn. I must in some way have come upon the trail of the Headsman, to cause him to strike at me like this."

Flynn looked at him, wordlessly, dropped the broken cuff-link into his vest pocket.

"I say the Headsman," Wentworth went on slowly, "because his is the only criminal trail I could have crossed recently, the only enemy I might have who could have contrived this thing."

"Tremaine James with Glastonbury?" Flynn queried.

Wentworth nodded. "At the Ranfair, yes. But I doubt if he knows anything. Probably an innocent tool. He would be too obviously a suspect. It goes deeper than that." He laughed shortly. "No, Flynn, there's nothing I can say, no clue I can give you."

HE PICKED up his glass again, quickly tossed off what remained.

He was trapped. There was no doubt about that. He even had a sudden premonition that other information would strengthen the evidence against him as time went on. He recalled Nita's fears. He was, in fact, at a loss to account for his own calmness. He knew that his pulses were throbbing with heavy hard strokes, but the glass in his hand was absolutely steady.

Flynn arose sharply, like the unfolding of a long carpenter's ruler.

"I believe you," he said slowly, as Wentworth stood also. "But my opinion doesn't matter. Have to ask you to stay in town."

Wentworth's surprise showed in his face. "That's white of you, Flynn, not arresting me," he said, "but I don't want you to make trouble for yourself."

Flynn made a jerky negative motion with one of his shapely hands. "My business," he said. "Advise you to get busy. Catch Headsman." His smile was wintry. He offered his firm, youthful hand for a warm clasp—and the next instant was striding, long-legged, from the room.

Conley was on his feet, too, now. "He *is* a white guy!" he exclaimed.

Wentworth stared thoughtfully at the floor, rubbed a heavy hand across his eyes.

"There's a catch in it somewhere," he said slowly. "A hole in the evidence, or he wouldn't have done it. Flynn is friendly, but also, like my friend Kirkpatrick before him, he performs his duty to the last degree." He smiled faintly, met Conley's direct blue gaze. "Well, you're answered about Kentucky. I've got to stay here and...."

Wentworth's eyes narrowed. The smile on his lips tightened and became menacing.

"By all the gods," he swore softly. "That's exactly what the Headsman means me to do! This was a move either to kill me or keep me out of the fight in Kentucky! Running away will condemn me, but... Jenkyns! Jenkyns! Get Ram Singh! I'm flying west in half an hour!"

87

CHAPTER 9
FEARFUL NEWS

THE HOT noon sun was blazing overhead when Wentworth set his plane down on the field at Paducah, Kentucky. The turf thereabouts was brown and dry. Leaves hung listlessly on the trees. It was as if the fear of people had communicated itself to nature and blighted the vegetation. The mechanics, who took the ship in charge and wheeled it toward the tarmac, moved heavily.

A taxi, driven by a Negro, whirled them at frantic speed over winding hill road and presently they were rolling up the tree-lined streets of Horton. There were glimpses of white facades behind high shrubbery, places which should have been peaceful and filled with a delicate southern charm. But here and there along the way were blank lots with ash-filled pits in their midsts, which also had been homes. About them, the trees were withered and charred.

At the hotel, no more actually than a large boarding house, the long, high-ceilinged dining-room was fanned by the rhythmic revolution of overhead fans. Awnings shaded the windows. The service of the smiling old Negro waiter was unobtrusive, but Wentworth scarcely noticed these things. He was nearly through with luncheon when Jackson strode into the room, his sharp eyes questing over the tables. He marched up to Wentworth, clicked heels with a military precision which was almost a salute. His light-colored palm beach suit had great splotches of dampness upon the shoulders.

"Anything to report, Jackson?"

"Yes, Major!" Suppressed excitement lay in Jackson's voice, but he said nothing further, and Wentworth, lifting his own eyes, saw that the other wished to report privately. He nodded.

"Very well, Jackson. Get something to eat and come to my room in half an hour—if your report can wait."

Jackson pivoted and marched from the room. "A man of incalculable value," Wentworth told Ron Conley softly. "Keen and brave and, above all things, loyal."

Conley's eyes were upon his plate. His lips stirred in a faintly mocking smile. "I can appreciate loyalty," he said slowly. "One feels the lack of it." His words were tinged with bitterness, but Wentworth, knowing that he referred to the fact that people he had counted his friends had turned against him, did not comment.

"I'd like to have some detailed information about the gold mining activities of this man, Taliaferro," Wentworth said. "You say his holdings are extensive. I'd like to know their exact location, the names of competitors and so on."

Conley agreed eagerly, eyes speculatively on Wentworth's face as he told what he knew.

"Masters is out in the hills, I believe," Wentworth said next.

Conley nodded. "So I was told. He's leading a party of militia who are hunting for the beast-men."

"Has Beth Welver had any word from her father?"

Conley shook his head slowly. "I don't know, sir. The house was closed when I went by there last. Beth is visiting some relatives in Coonville, over the mountain."

WENTWORTH SAT staring at his plate. He had raced away from New York under the certain belief that the criminals behind the raids of the beast-men, presumably the Headsman, did not want him in Kentucky. But now that he was here, there seemed nothing active that could be done. Tracking the men through the hills would not help. The bone-dry earth, baked by the burning sun, would not betray their passage, nor hold a scent long enough for dogs to follow. Moreover, it seemed unlikely that the criminals behind the attacks would lay themselves open to capture by remaining with the beast-men. And yet, *somewhere* about here must lie the trail. Perhaps Taliaferro....

On the point of leaving the dining-room Wentworth checked rigidly, then strode toward the door with both hands extended.

"Nita!" he cried. "What in the world...."

She smiled at him cheerfully. She wore a linen suit of light blue which fitted her exquisitely modeled body to perfection, and the light straw upon her head was rakish. She accepted his hands.

"I've been needing a holiday," she declared. "A bit of hunting seemed a good idea, somehow." Her lips were still smiling, but there was a quick warning in her eyes.

Wentworth kissed each of her hands in turn, then rapped sharply on the reception desk in the hall for the boarding-house proprietor. He directed the man to take Nita's registry. Afterward, he excused himself from Conley and escorted her upstairs—conscious of the disapproving scowl of the bewhiskered proprietor. Behind the door of Nita's room, he gathered her close into his arms.

"But why, darling, did you come out here?" he demanded. "You know there's terrible danger here. There's no way of telling when these Neanderthalers will strike, and when they do...." Anger and apprehension alike hardened the muscles of his shoulders.

"Dick! You're cracking my ribs!"

He released her with a smile. "You had something to tell me?" Her face sobered.

"Yes. I called Kirkpatrick as you asked and told him you wanted him, as governor, to delay any extradition moves if possible until you could get to the bottom of this mystery."

She moved close again and twisted the lapels of his coat in agitated, small white fists. "Dick, he said it was impossible! He sounded very worried and anxious and advised you to return to New York at once."

Wentworth's face was expressionless, except that the tight hard lines now invested the corners of his eyes again.

"And when you told him that was impossible?" he prompted.

Nita shook her head, her deep violet eyes studying his. "Dick," she whispered. "He said you'd better stay in New York and bend all your efforts toward smashing the evidence against you. He said that once you... you were convicted, it would be useless to look to him for help."

"The devil!" Wentworth was startled. He had not expected ever to appeal to Kirkpatrick in that way, but the governor's assumption of conviction was a little ominous. Could fresh evidence have developed?

To his quick question, Nita shook her head. "Not that I know of," she replied. "None that was printed in the papers, at any rate. I don't think your absence has been discovered yet, Dick. Maybe… maybe you'd better go back and try to destroy this frame-up."

Her voice was hopeless even as she said it. She knew Wentworth never considered himself until after the enemies of mankind had been destroyed. In his strong sure knowledge of innocence, he attached little importance to any plot against himself.

EVEN NOW he was shaking his head slowly. "I can't go back, dearest. That's precisely what the men behind all this villainy *want* me to do. If Kirkpatrick is warning me, there must be much more to the case than I thought. And I know enough about courts to realize that innocence is no presumption of acquittal. The present district attorney, Youngwell, was a protégé of Glastonbury. It would be splendid political capital for him to avenge his friend. Yes, Kirkpatrick's wise."

He stood pondering. "Better get a nap, darling," he said then, gently. "I know you were up most of the night waiting to hear the results of the duel. There won't be any danger until tonight, that's certain. By that time, I'll be with you." He gathered her once more in his arms, and then left.

In his room, Jackson was waiting for him. The ex-sergeant sprang at once to his feet, his face dark and frowning.

"Major, I think Conley is mixed up with this thing," he declared vigorously. "At any rate, his girl, Beth Welver, is. She had a ticket to go on that bus that the beast-men wrecked. At the last minute, she got a telegram… she was already on the bus.

She grabbed her bag and stopped the bus. Got off and ran like she was scared. The bus had no more than got clear of the town than it was rushed and everybody on board killed."

Wentworth frowned, dragged a palm across his forehead. He stood very straight, in the middle of the room, hands hanging idly at his sides. Slowly he thought over every aspect of the girl's connection with the trouble. Her rescue from the first Horton raid by Masters, her father's disappearance, her flight from the bus.

"How about Masters?" he asked slowly.

Jackson shook his head vehemently. "He's been helping against the raids, sir. Following trails, leading defenses. Don't think there's any chance, sir. He's the one responsible for Conley bringing you back out here."

Wentworth nodded slowly. "Keep Beth Welver under surveillance then," he said. "She's supposed to be at the home of relatives in Coonville. Call the house and check on her movements for the afternoon… Tell Ram Singh I want him to stand guard over *Missie sahib*… with—his—life. And, until we form contact with Beth Welver, you keep an eye on Conley."

Jackson saluted, as always when in private, and strode from the room. Wentworth crossed to the shaded window and stared down at the sun-drenched street. No one moved. A hound drowsed half under the porch, twitched a muscle to stir a fly. The room was close and Wentworth peeled off his coat, draped his shoulder-holster guns over the bed post, flung himself down in hope of managing a nap. His mind had been too stirred throughout the flight west; he was heavy with fatigue.

Twilight lay in a lavender shadow across the floor when he awoke and realized presently that a knock—repeated sharply as he lay there—had aroused him. He arose swiftly, buckled on his holsters and got into his coat as he went to the door.

Jackson came in. His wide-jawed face was taut with drawn muscles and his eyes looked frightened.

"Beth Welver just got off the bus here in Horton," he said hoarsely. "I tried all afternoon to get her in Coonville. Her relatives said she was downtown somewhere—then she gets off the bus here. They didn't know she was leaving, Major, and that means...."

His voice faded as Wentworth nodded sharply. "If your previous deductions are correct, Jackson, it means that the Neanderthal hordes will attack Coonville tonight." His lips thinned, pressed hard against his teeth. If it was a smile, it was not a pretty one. "Jackson, I think we shall request the honor of Miss Welver's company on a little automobile ride."

Jackson's expression did not lighten. He stood awaiting orders.

"Get a car, a fast closed car," Wentworth said. "Have it in front of the hotel in fifteen minutes."

A HALF hour later, Wentworth sat carelessly in the back of the car beside Beth Welver while Jackson sent it rapidly up a mountain road the slope of which began to rise steeply before they had ever left the environs of Horton. Beth sat stiffly erect, her hands knotted in her lap, her blue eyes wide and frightened. The hot wind stirred her long golden hair, done in coronet braids about her head.

"Where are we going, Mr. Wentworth?" Her words issued between hurried breaths.

Wentworth turned his head toward her, and smiled slowly. "Just for a little ride, Miss Welver." His voice was light.

The girl subsided, but her hands twisted more restlessly in her lap. Her eyes flicked to the roadside scenery, the dry shrubbery now being colored to softer shades by the dying light. Still the car hissed upward, the valley beginning to drop below them. Houses down there were marked by mere pinpricks of illumination.

"Mr. Wentworth." The girl's voice was shrill. "It's dangerous on these roads at night. The beast-men...."

"We're going quite rapidly," Wentworth said calmly, "and we won't stop until we reach Coonville...."

"Coonville!" She jerked out the word.

"Why, yes, Coonville. It's a nice town, isn't it?"

The girl's head twisted awkwardly toward him. The tension of her neck muscles made her throat line ugly, and her mouth was open a little, her eyes dark with fear. Her head began to shake slowly from side to side.

"No, No. *No!*" Her voice soared. "Not Coonville. We can't go to Coonville!"

"I see nothing against it," Wentworth said evenly.

She seized his arm with both hands. Her words stumbled over one another in frantic utterance. They had no meaning except that she did not wish to go to Coonville.

Wentworth still displayed smiling lips, but there was an ugly gleam in his eyes. He tore the girl's hand loose from his arm and thrust her violently from him, so that she slumped down in her corner. There she half lay, half sat, motionless, eyes closed, moaning a little now and again through pale lips.

"I'm through… through," she declared. "Father would not want me to help you… even as much as I have. Now you're breaking your promise… taking me back to die… at the hands of beasts…."

Wentworth studied her face attentively. She was saying in effect that she believed him to be connected with whoever was behind the beast-men. And that reference to her father….

"Do you know where your father is?" he asked.

The girl's eyes opened. "You know I don't," she said bitterly. "All I know is that he's in your power, and that you'll probably kill him when you don't need my information any longer."

"You work for the railroad, don't you, Miss Welver?"

"I work for you!" Her voice was bitter.

WENTWORTH NODDED slowly. The picture began to take shape. The killers were holding the girl's father a hostage for her to continue supplying information about rich trains to be looted. They had warned her when a raid of the beast-men threatened—not so much to save her as to protect a source of information. And she was prevented from revealing her knowledge of impending raids by the fact that they held her father hostage. Greater persons than Beth Welver might have weakened and yielded under that suasion.

"At what time is the attack on Coonville planned?" Wentworth asked sharply.

The girl rolled her head on the cushions. "You should know that better than I," she said.

"You mean that you don't know?"

"I don't know anything," Beth declared angrily. She sat erect and glared at Wentworth. "You give me warnings just in time to get clear of a place which I know will be raided within a few hours by those beasts. I know that the women I see may be horribly murdered, that the men may be torn to pieces by the hands of those damnable men. Yet I can't open my mouth—if I do… if I do…."

Her head sagged. The courage and the stiffness went out of her, and sobs jerked at her shoulders. "I can't stand it," she gasped. "I can't. I'm going to warn the people in Coonville. Father would want me to do that."

Wentworth nodded his head. "Just so," he said. "If I'm not mistaken there's a house with a phone on top of the mountain. We can send a warning from there."

She snapped up her head, her eyes widely incredulous. "You— you'll warn Coonville?"

Wentworth smiled and nodded again. "Quite. I am more anxious than you could possibly be to give the warning."

Beth Welver shook her golden head slowly, choked on a sob.

He explained to her, then, how he had become suspicious of the fact that she had fled from the doomed bus. And finally he convinced her that he was battling to save, not destroy, people. Then he besought information about her father.

"There isn't much to tell," she said presently. "Father was gone when I came back to the village after those… those *things* carried me off. I didn't know what had happened to him until I went to work the next day. Somebody cut in on my wire—I'm a telegrapher—and tapped out to me the information that my father was in the hands of the beast-men, but that nothing would happen to him if I told no one and if I obeyed orders."

Afterward, by the same medium, she went on, had come orders that she was to report, when next the telegraph instrument sounded, the time and value of various freight shipments. Even when the trains were wrecked and looted, she had not been able to bring herself to cause her father's death by telling what she knew. All attempts to trace down the spot where the wire was tapped had failed. And then had come the warning that she was to leave Coonville....

Jackson pulled the car to a halt before a large, unlighted log cabin at the crest of the mountain. There was a porch and tables under the trees. Evidently it was a mountain-top roadhouse. But there was no sign of human residents at present. Jackson's heavy pounding on the door brought no response, and finally they smashed in a window, found the telephone. It was beside a window from which Wentworth could see, far below, the twinkling light of two towns; Horton to the north, Coonville to the south. Soon horror and desolation would strike down there....

He lifted the receiver and whirled the crank vigorously. But he knew even before the bell had died that it was useless. The receiver he held to his ear was absolutely dead. Savagely, he whirled from the instrument.

"We've got to get to Coonville in nothing flat," he snapped at

Jackson. "The phone in there is dead, and the horde may attack at any moment."

HE HURDLED through the window he had smashed, sprang to the car, and Jackson had it rolling instantly, head-lights tunneling whitely through the thick night. Frequently the beams thrust straight out over space as the car spun around hairpin turns. Wentworth seized the emergency strap and hung on, but Beth Welver seemed not to care. She lay laxly against the cushions, rolling with every wild lurch of the sedan.

Jackson was tense above the steering wheel. Now and again his shoulders hunched in sudden tension as he jockeyed the yawing machine around a sharp curve. The road was buttressed with white crash fences, guaranteed to stop a car at any normal speed.

But they were not traveling at normal speed. A miss, a skid, a weakened steering knuckle, and the car would dive out into space, carrying to destruction not only three souls, but the whole of the unsuspecting town of Coonville in the valley below. For the warning must be given....

Wentworth's eyes were narrowed in thought as he swayed with the lurching of the car. All this information seemed an added link in the evidence against Taliaferro. But Taliaferro as well could be only a cog—unless, indeed, he had criminal subordinates in New York. Wentworth reflected bitterly that Taliaferro was more apt to have superiors there... A more violent lurch wrenched his attention to the speeding car.

Thirty miles an hour was a suicidal pace on this torturous road, writhing like a wounded snake across the precipitous mountainside. For fifty feet the road would slant across the decline, then, like a frightened rabbit, double back upon itself causing Jackson to jam on shrieking brakes, fight the lunging car, and skitter about the turn with only inches between the wheels and black destruction. Curve followed curve in dizzying succession.

Then it happened. They were halfway down and in the very midst of a slamming, brake-ripping curve, when the right rear tire went. Its blast was a muffled hiss of air.

The sedan lurched wildly, and the other rear tire exploded. On bare rims, the car shrilled across the road, hit the crash fence in a skid, teetered on the brink of a cliff the tree-bristling bottom of which was lost in black depths.

"Out, Jackson," Wentworth barked.

His right hand flew to the door. His left caught Beth Welver by the arm. He saw Jackson hurl from behind the wheel and at the same instant the car stopped its teetering, lurched defiantly toward the cliff. Over the uplifting running board Wentworth sprang, dragging the girl with him. He sprawled headlong into the road, the girl plunging bodily on top of him. There was a rasp of metal as the car took off, then silence—silence for a breath-catching instant, followed by a dim, distant crash of smashed metal and glass. To their ears came a second explosive crash, then there was silence again—this time finally.

Wentworth picked himself up stiffly. Jackson was beside him instantly, and between them, they lifted Beth Welver to her feet. She began to laugh weakly, sagging against their arms for support. Her laughter grew more shrill. Sharply they shook her out of the fit of hysteria.

"Take charge of her, Jackson," Wentworth ordered. "I'm going ahead to the village."

He darted off at a steady jogging run before Jackson could protest. It would take forty or forty-five minutes to reach the village if he ran into no other obstacles, such as a raiding party of beast-men. And it was growing late. Darkness did not fall until around eight o'clock. An hour had elapsed since then. It would be ten o'clock when he reached Coonville, and in these towns, ten o'clock meant all lights out—a time ripe for the attack of the beast-men.

At the thought, he unconsciously lengthened his stride. But then he forced himself to a saner pace. As he ran, he ripped off his coat, tossed it to the side of the road. His automatics still nestled in their arm holsters. He was grimly glad of them, glad even of their weight against his body as he ran.

Death was in their weight and, by the heavens, he would need death as an ally this night!

CHAPTER 10
THE BEAST-MEN ATTACK

A T FIRST, Wentworth ran without conscious effort. It was all down hill and the road was smooth asphalt. But the curves were maddening. He traveled fifty yards, and he had advanced only ten toward the helpless town below. The ravines between the curves were deep; choked with shrubbery and jagged rock. There was no help for it.

He ran with his head thrown back, his arms lifted, fists clenched. The gun belts hampered his movements somewhat, but those guns meant power, power against the hordes that were coming. Five miles to go… Time after time he fought down his tendency to sprint. He could never last it out that way. But the urge of the hill was under his heels. It tipped him forward, persistently stepped up his pace.

Now and again, through the thick drought-browned foliage, he could spot the gleam of the town's lights. No automobiles passed. No man ventured out of his home these nights. Men sat behind locked doors, barricaded windows, with rifles at their elbows. Much good that would do them. One rifle in a house, two or three even, would not stop these hordes; no, nor a half dozen, before the beast-men broke in and killed, killed, killed.

When the snake-writhing road finally straightened out into the last good stretch toward town, Wentworth's breath was coming in gasps between his teeth. He was drenched with sweat, there was a heaviness in his legs. He could run ten miles at a reasonable pace, but his pace had not been reasonable.

About him the night was close and hot. The sky was thick with clouds and not a breath of moving air disturbed the brittle foliage at the road side. Not a sound in all the world except the spurning rasp of his feet, the gasp of his pumping breath. And the town still a mile away.

Now he ran with legs driven by will alone, now that his strength was dwindling. Years ago up there on the mountain there had been knife thrusts of pain in his side, but he had ignored them and now they were no more. Something else was bothering him. Would he have the breath to sound the alarm when he reached Coonville, stretching out ahead with its meager pattern of street lights, and shuttered windows showing, here and there, thin lines of yellow lamp-gleam?

The road extended as straight as a bullet at last, a narrow black strip of smooth pavement stretching on and on. The number of times he picked up his feet and drove them down one before the other seemed unending. He seemed to stand still, the lights drawing no nearer. Persistently his mind reverted to the mathematics of his running. Each pace was seven feet—no, that wasn't likely. He was tired. His stride was probably five feet now—perhaps even four. At that rate it would take a thousand, a thousand or more strides before he reached that first outflung village light. A thousand driving efforts of will. He began to count his paces... *one... two... three...* How far beyond the lights were the first houses? Would there be a phone from which the alarm could be spread?... *eight... nine... ten....*

As in a nightmare, he heard a dull thumping, like the beat of a muted drum, which kept time with his feet... *eleven... twelve... thirteen...* A hoarse roaring scream half beastlike, half human, split the night!

The scream of a beast-man who had made a kill!

WENTWORTH FALTERED in his stride. His feet seemed suddenly unable to keep pace with his body. He was too late then, too late. The beast-men had struck. That scream had given the warning that he should have given an hour before.

His feet stumbled. Instinctively, he balled as he fell, landed rolling on his back, came back to his feet with a dull throbbing ache in his shoulders. He plunged on, staring toward the clustered lights ahead.

Everything was as before. No flames lit the night sky, there were no more screams, either of triumphant killer or fleeing victim. Almost he convinced himself that the hoarse roar had been the product of his overwrought imagination. He began to hope again. Perhaps, perhaps he would be in time....

The thing arose from the ditch beside the road and began to run soundlessly behind him. It overhauled him with long, easy strides. Wentworth was stumbling, panting with his efforts. He was running headlong, with no thought now of husbanding his strength. His breath was heavy and hot in his throat. The rasp of it drowned out the slight scrape of feet behind him. In its right hand the beast-man clutched a heavy sledge, in its left a short, thick spear.

As it ran, the thing began to make small chuckling noises in its throat and it was this that finally reached Wentworth's ears. Numb with fatigue, he twisted about, saw the great beast shadow at his heels, striding along with enormous vitality, with easy strength, chuckling in an anticipation of slaughter. In each hand a weapon which could smash a man into instant death. And he had only his guns, guns that would be useless against that hulk. Even his superior agility had been sapped by long exertion.

But he stopped, whipped out his guns, and faced the creature. It stopped also, then, standing with both weapons and hands hanging; a hunch-shouldered thing of enormous power, an overgrown gorilla of a man. The thing's lips skinned back from its teeth in a guttural snarl. The teeth gleamed.

Wentworth's chest was laboring mightily. He fought for breath. But suddenly he caught that breath in his throat and loosed a shout as hoarse and challenging as any beast-killer's cry! Then he sprang straight toward the crouching monster!

For an instant, the thing stood there, staring stupidly, mouthing ominous sounds. Then it, too, sounded a hoarse roar. Whipping both hammer and spear above its head, it leaped forward, and hurled the spear straight at Wentworth.

They were twenty feet apart Wentworth barely shrank aside from the hideous weapon. He heard it whistle with the speed of its passage. But he did not hesitate in his own charge. His guns were ready in both hands. He made no effort to fire. The shock of a bullet, hitting in the right spot, might shake the monster for a moment. It could not stop him.

With a final, leaping spring, the thing lunged toward him. Once more Wentworth sprang aside, heard the down-sweeping hammer clash on the road, saw sparks fly.

He had accomplished his purpose now. He was behind the thing. Whirling so close against the monster that his chest almost touched its back he lifted his automatic and pumped hot lead into the base of the creature's skull, shattering the spine, driving lead through the thick bone which encased the brain. For fully thirty seconds he stood there firing, then sprang backward and, whirling, sprinted madly up the road.

THAT BATTERING discharge of lead should have killed any mortal thing. But these beasts had incredible vitality. Twisting his head about, Wentworth saw the creature swing about, start after him with great lunging strides. It did not scream now. But its hand still clutched the deadly hammer.

Two, three, four huge strides the thing took. The hammer flew from its hand with devilish accuracy. Wentworth plunged aside, watched as it took two more leaping strides.

And all at once the creature went limp, in the air. It hit the road with terrific force, rolled over twice, and lay motionless, flat on its back, its arms and legs flung wide.

Chest heaving, hands clutched convulsively about the butts of his automatic—one of which was almost empty—Wentworth stood there, staring. Then, methodically, he stuffed fresh cartridges into the gun and walked back toward the thing he had slain. His feet dragged heavily.

His lips twisted in a wry grin. This would be a hell of a thing on which to put the Spider seal. The seal would mean nothing to the beast-men. The leaders, if they saw it, would laugh and think the Spider stooped low these days for his kill.

For a moment, he paused to stare down at the creature. The snarling face was horrible. Bullets had created a shambles where they had smashed out, with explosive force, through the flesh.

Wentworth turned his head toward the city and marched on, eyes alertly scanning the roadside ditches. He heard screams now, screams of men dying, and screams of bestial triumph. A red glow simmered against the sky off to the right of the road he followed. It brightened, then a tongue of yellow flame licked upward.

Far ahead, where that first outpost of light stood timorously against the dark, a hulking, stooped shadow showed for an instant, lumbering forward toward the trees which lined the street. Wentworth ran on heavily. No need now to hurry, to shout a warning. The town was in arms, barricaded, and aware… here and there beast-men were already smashing through all obstacles, as despairing cries indicated.

What could one lone man do, armed with weapons which must be emptied at close range, in a precise spot, to kill—and which still might not be enough to stop the victim from slaying his conqueror? Wentworth might have appropriated that sledge hammer. If he used it with all his force, it might smash a head.

His wry smile still twitched his lips. He moved with horror, for he knew what was being enacted where the beast-men made breaches in the walls. The flame of anger rose inside him with a slow, increasing incandescence. The fighting rage of the Spider, the rage which ever arose when he knew innocent people were being destroyed at the behest of megalomaniac leaders of the criminal world. Such a rage as had driven him from the first time he had killed—for the sake of humanity.

He walked openly down the road now, making no effort at all to hide. He stalked past the hot white hole the first light made in the darkness, where a few minutes before a beast-man had paused clenching primitive spear and deadly sledge. Sooner or later, he would meet one of those horrors, and then… and then….

THE BEAST-MAN did not see Wentworth. It was intent on a thin thread of light which slid out beneath a battered window. Now and again the creature lifted its head and sniffed

107

like a dog. There was whimpering eagerness in its throat, a sound that made his skin tauten behind Wentworth's ears, sent a prickling over his scalp. He had heard dogs whimper like that, stud dogs at mating time.

He lifted a wetted finger to the wind and found that the drift was from the house toward himself. He nodded. His lips were no longer smiling. They were drawn back in a snarl as that beast-thing's had been. There was a primal rage within him, a stiffness in his knees as he stalked this semi-human prey. The beast had a heavy double-bitted woodsman's axe that he wanted. This was how primeval man had behaved—slipping up behind an enemy to kill for the sake of a coveted weapon.

The thing's ears would be as keen as a wild thing's, Wentworth knew. Thus he stalked it as he would have stalked a tiger in its native jungle—his guns ready, his teeth bared. The fire of his anger was burning within him.

He got within ten feet of the thing before it sensed his presence and whirled with the speed of steel springs uncoiling. Wentworth roared a challenge and rushed. As that other beast-man had been, this one too was stunned at the charge. It was used to fleet-footed fear in its foes, and its mind, though attuned to swift combat, could not readily accept a new idea. Fear of this charging creature, surprise, rage, mingled in its slow brain.

As Wentworth swept in, the creature swung up the double-bitted axe as lightly as a man might lift a foil. It swept the weapon in a wide, sideward arc. Wentworth went under the swing on one knee, came up behind the creature—and once more his gun blasted its rapid roll of death. He darted around a corner of the house and waited while the creature screamed out its death agonies. There was a thunderous sound of wood yielding beneath the blows of the axe, the blasting of a rifle, finally silence.

Wentworth crept back around the corner of the house. In its final agonies the beast-man had nearly wrecked the frame of a window and the weatherboarding beneath it.

He slipped close, caught up the heavy axe, the primitive spear as well, and ran lightly away. His reloaded automatics were in their holsters. His lungs no longer pumped from the exertion of his long run; swiftly his marvelously attuned body was regaining its strength.

He moved more rapidly now. He had bested two of the beast-men, slain them with difficulty and danger it was true—but slain them. And now he had weapons better suited to the combat.

He turned a corner, saw bright flames lick eagerly up the tinder-dry side of a frame house. Three of the beast-men danced excitedly in the light of the fire and from within the house rose screams. Through a window a rifle began to speak deliberately. Wentworth heard the pain-inspired roar of one of the beast-men, saw its arm whip forward. A throwing stone smashed through the boarding over the window where the gun had been fired. The rifle did not speak again.

Now the creatures began to run in leaping circles about the house, their faces, with vicious eyes and snarling teeth, turned always toward the building. The cries within the house were those of women. An upper window was flung open and Wentworth saw a girl, her dark hair streaming about her face, look out and then give vent to scream after frenzied scream.

CHAPTER 11
WITH STONE-AGE WEAPONS

THE BEAST-MEN made no effort to cast their weapons at the girl. Merely they danced, while guttural sounds, little whining eager noises came from their throats.

Another girl came behind the one in the window now, and with her was an older woman. The latter had a rifle, and driving the girls back she crouched and aimed at the three excitedly dancing figures below.

It was a scene out of a dark and fearsome past. The woman fired and a beast-man raised a fearful snarling. He ran toward the house, sprang upward, caught hold of a blind and climbed, ravening, toward the window. The woman leaned out and pointed her rifle directly at the thing's face.

Wentworth saw another of the beast-men draw back his spear. He snatched out an automatic, snapped a quick shot that way. He made no effort to kill the creature. His bullet pierced the arm which gripped the spear. The weapon was already being launched, javelin-like, but the shot spoiled its aim. It crashed against the side of the house and smashed through wood, burying its head there quiveringly. The woman at the window fired straight down into the breast of the savage half-beast clinging to the side of the house, fired again and again while the girls shrieked and fought to pull her back to safety.

Up, up, in the face of each savagely beating slug, the beast-thing climbed. It grasped the muzzle of the rifle with a powerful hand and ripped it from the woman's hands. Then it slammed the weapon at her like a club. The blow caught her on the side of the head and sent her reeling from the window. Wentworth knew that the force of it had smashed her skull.

Curses were pouring from his lips. But he knew the futility of attacking openly against three beast-men. One he might handle, but three…. He crouched, and resting his automatic against the side of the tree began a slow, deliberate fire at the creature above.

He did not aim at the thing's head or body, but discharged bullet after bullet at the right arm, by which the thing clung to the second story framework. Finally that arm sagged help-lessly. The creature was shrieking with pain and rage. Yet it still hung by its prehensile feet, grasping a lower section. It banged the rifle against the side of the house in its anger. Deliberately, Wentworth began to fire at its legs.

Flames were leaping higher than the roof now, a torch of defiance against the sky. Windows had long ago burst under the heat. Smoke began to dribble out on all sides.

The beast-men danced more wildly. They seemed to disre-gard the attack upon one of their number, once more took up their exultant leaping circle about the house. Wentworth fired four shots into the left leg of the creature clinging to the cornice before, with a roar which drowned even the crackle of flames, it pitched to the earth, falling awkwardly on its head and then lying quite still.

The girls were at the window again, one staring behind in

terror, the other gazing with horrorstruck eyes at the prancing beasts below. The flames threw lurid light into the room. Both girls wore their night clothing.

WENTWORTH'S AUTOMATICS were emptied and he filled one, then found that in his running and battling he had lost the rest of his bullets. Well, the automatic might account for one of those creatures.

He crouched again behind the tree and aimed at the legs of the nearest of the two beasts. He was on the point of firing when there was a rending and rumbling. He jerked up his eyes to find that part of the wall of the house had fallen inward. The flames leaped with a higher, more exultant abandon. The girls hugged each other in terror, then darted away from the window. A moment later, the front door opened and the larger girl, with her dark hair about her shoulders, stepped out.

She was alone, and the high leaping flames spotlighted her gracefully rounded body against the dark front of the house.

For an instant the beast-things stood staring. Then, with resounding roars, they leaped forward. Wentworth's breath caught in his throat as he realized the magnanimity of the girl's action. She was sacrificing herself to the beasts so that her younger sister might escape—walking steadily forward, across the porch, to meet the creatures' rush. Her expression was like that of a sleepwalker.

Wentworth stepped clear of the tree, lifted his automatic and fired with the slow, deliberate measure of the pistol range. His bullets ticked like clockwork into the right leg of the nearest beast-man. At his fourth shot, the creature pitched to the ground, but still crawled forward, snarling horribly.

Catching up both axe and spear in one hand, Wentworth gripped the automatic in the other and charged forward. The remaining beast had reached the porch. With effortless ease, it sprang over the railing, reached out a long hairy arm and scooped the girl close into his embrace. Wentworth saw her body go limp. He threw back his head and hurled the challenging cry for the beast-men into the night air. For a moment the thing was too intent upon its prize to hear, but when he roared it out again it pulled its bestial head about and stared toward where he charged across the fire-lit lawn.

The beast-man whose leg had been broken reared up in Wentworth's path. Swaying on one foot, its smashed leg dangling, it lifted the spear above its head with both hands.

Wentworth leaped close, fired his last two bullets into its forehead at point blank range. The next instant he was past while the thing still reeled on its one leg.

It could not pursue, handicapped as it was by that broken leg. Its screams soared to the heavens, but Wentworth was already approaching the porch. He stopped his mad charge and stalked, stiff-kneed, toward the one remaining beast-man. The thing held the girl's now naked body in one arm and brandished a sledge with the other. Its hoarse, roaring challenge was continuous and Wentworth imitated it. His useless automatic had been shoved back into its holster. He thrust the axe through his belt and held the spear ready in both hands.

Wentworth bounded forward
in a long, furious dive aimed
at the spear-end protruding
from the beastman's back.

"You in the house!" he shouted. "When I make this beast drop your sister, come and drag her away. Understand?"

A GIRL'S voice came weakly from within, agreeing, and Wentworth hurled another taunting roar at the beast. He jerked the spear overhead with both hands as if to hurl it squarely at the creature.

The feint succeeded. With an answering roar which fairly

shook the house, the thing dropped the girl and whipped up its left arm protectively. Frantically it flailed the hammer, which swept down, and missed Wentworth as he swayed out of the way. With all the weight of his body behind, Wentworth lunged with the spear, aiming low at the pit of the stomach where the ribs separated.

The creature's left arm swept down and hit the point. Powerful as was Wentworth's thrust, the sweep of the thing's arm almost turned the blow, spoiled its aim, so that the point barely ripped its side. That single blow almost ended the fight for Wentworth. For no sooner had the beast swept down with its left hand than the hammer was whipped up again with a force which, with the merest brush of its steel head, would have smashed every bone in his body. He never knew how he evaded the weapon and leaped back to safety.

He realized that he was no match for this beast in agility. But the dangling spear hampered the creature. It paused for an instant to snatch the point out and hurl the weapon angrily away. A gush of blood followed its plucking but the wound, which would have laid an ordinary man unconscious on the earth, appeared merely to infuriate it. Wentworth stared into its low-browed face, the feral eyes burning redly beneath the bony ridges of the brows, the mobile flaps of lips snarling away from long yellow teeth, and a wave of uncertainty washed coldly over his body.

Who was he to think that he could kill this animal thing out of the past? What were his weak human theories against the incredible brute force of this creature, with muscles which rippled like giant constrictors under its skin? Nevertheless he swept up his hammer again. He did not know the meaning of fear.

He did a strange thing. As the beast charged upon him with

great, bounding leaps and upraised hammer, he laughed. Flung laughter like a challenge into the beast's face—then leaped forward, too. In his two hands he held the double-bitted axe, even as the beast held the hammer.

Out of the corner of his eye, he glimpsed the figure of the second girl slipping out of the door toward where her sister's unconscious body lay, just out of the reach of the battle. The girl had come too soon. The beast-man could reach them in a leap. With a sweep of that sledge, he could crush the life from both. Only Wentworth's charge prevented their instantaneous annihilation.

The beast-man's eyes were small and murderous. The creature welcomed the charge, set itself to meet the rush of this puny thing which dared to attack.

But when the heavy hammer swept down, Wentworth was not there. He had checked his advance with one foot hitting the ground hard and, as the hammer swept past, he struck above it with a hurried motion half jab, half hack. One of the razor-edged bits of the axe sank deep into the bicep muscle of the beast's left arm. Then he danced away.

He wanted to gash the creature's throat, sever the arm from the shoulder, but there had not been time. It was the blow he had struck or nothing. When he retreated, he moved away from the porch. The girls were still there. Damn it, why didn't she get her sister away? If his foot slipped, if he miscalculated for an instant, they were all three doomed!

THE BEAST-THING was whimpering with pain now. Wentworth's slash had partly crippled its left arm. But it was

117

plain that he had not entirely severed the muscle for the creature could still lift the arm. The rage of the thing was beyond anything Wentworth had ever seen. Its teeth champed out foam. All semblance of humanness had been stripped away. It was simply a beast fighting for its prey, a beast challenged by another beast. But Wentworth was a thinking beast. He planned....

Coolly, as he had awaited the charge of that rogue elephant in the jungle once, he awaited the charge now. He did not pull back the axe above his head. He held it poised before him like a bayonet, both hands gripping the haft.

The beast-man came in, waddling on bent, cautious legs, head thrust forward, hammer poised. From nearly ten feet away it leaped, slashing downward with the sledge.

Wentworth did not attempt to block the blow entirely. He knew it would shatter his axe, sweep the weapon from his hands. He struck the head of the sledge with the flat of his blade. Steel rang, the hammer was thrust aside.

The beast-man staggered, thrown half off balance by the shrewd blow. Wentworth leaped aside even as he fended and his axe, only half raised, slashed downward at the creature's leg. Once more the bit sliced home, and he sprang clear. He had not touched bone, but he had inflicted a great, gaping contusion. Blood was pouring from the creature's three wounds. Yet they did not dim its fury. The beast would keep coming as long as an ounce of life was left in its powerful tremendously vital body.

Wentworth chanced a quick glance toward the girls on the porch now, saw that both were on their feet. But still they had not fled. The elder girl had the heavy, blood-tipped spear in her hands, poised before her. She was a vision out of mythology, an unhelmeted Athena with the flame playing over her taut, rounded body.

Wentworth pulled his eyes back to the beast-man, sprang backward a yard to set himself, tripped… and fell! With a roar of triumph the beast leaped, hammer raised for the final, exterminating stroke.

The hammer swept down, a blurring black death. But Wentworth's eye had been trained on the floors of a thousand *salles d'armes*. Once more steel rang on steel, and the axe knocked the hammer aside. The beast-man did not attempt to lift it again. Foam slavering from its jaws, it hurled itself barehanded toward the Spider's prostrate form.

Wentworth set the butt of the axe upon the earth and rolled frantically to one side. The flat top of the steel head caught the beast-man across the chest, blocking his lumbering body for an instant. He plucked the axe aside, but Wentworth was clear, reeling to his feet six feet away. Then the axe whistled in a short arc through the air, squarely for Wentworth's head. With a desperate effort he dodged it, sprinted toward a tree. If he could keep out of reach of the creature….

HE HEARD a hoarse bellow of rage and pain, and he whirled—to see the beast turned from pursuit of himself and glaring toward the two girls on the porch. From its back protruded the haft and most of the point of the spear. The girl had hurled it true, though it had not penetrated far. And now they were fleeing. The younger one was just turning the corner of the blazing house. The elder ran lightly, watchfully behind her, not too fast. Also, she took a separate path, in order to lead the beast aside.

Wentworth ran after the axe and caught it up from where it had struck against a tree. Twice he whirled it about his head, then let it fly through the air, a glittering sparkle of light. Fast and true it sped toward the lumbering beast-man.

While it still was in the air Wentworth raced forward, caught up the twenty-pound sledge. It was nearly twice as heavy as the axe. He could swing it, but not with the speed of the axe—nor anything approaching the strength of the beast-man.

The axe caught the beast-man upon the shoulders and spilled it to the ground upon its face. The fleeing girl reached a tree and pivoted, staring back at the prone creature. The thing climbed groggily to its feet, turned heavily about. At last the steady drain of blood was telling upon its strength. Wentworth poised the heavy sledge and waited, the weapon drawn back, pillowed on his shoulder ready for use.

The beast no longer bellowed. Breath labored from its lungs. Yet no fatal wound had been inflicted. Eventually the creature might die of loss of blood, but even that was unlikely, at least soon.

Wentworth thought these things dimly as he watched the beast lumber toward him. There was still incredible strength in those gorilla arms, the hunched shoulders. Once the thing reached behind its back and plucked futilely at the prodding spear, could not quite reach it. Wentworth saw the girl creep from behind the tree and steal forward. Incredible courage in that slim unclad Athena. Loyal, too. Remaining to battle with the man who had come to her protection when she might have fled into the welcoming arms of the night.

This time Wentworth did not charge forward, but stood waiting. His weight was thrown forward on his toes, his shoulders swelled with the tension of muscles ready to strike.

When the beast was still ten feet away, he whipped the hammer forward, let go the haft, and sent it hurtling straight toward the creature's ugly face. The mighty arms came up and there was a thud, a snap. Then the creature's left arm hung useless at its side. Its right, however, grasped the hammer.

Snarling now, foaming with eagerness, the beast came raging toward the unarmed Wentworth. The hammer whipped through the air like a switch, reaching, reaching for this taunting, tiny man-thing which still defied its own mighty strength. Wentworth danced out of range. But the battle had taken toll of him, too. He had been near death there on the ground. He had barely dodged a half dozen fatal blows. Ever since he had fended that hammer with the axe, his arm had been heavy with numbness. And he had just run miles.

BUT HE kept out of the reach of the hammer and circled to get his axe. He saw that the girl was close to the weapon, had in fact caught it up and was racing forward to hand it to him. The beast-man noticed at the same instant and charged furiously. Wentworth danced wide, trying to lead the creature away from the girl—but for once the thing would not be decoyed. It swept on toward her, mouthing filthy sounds like obscene curses.

But now its back was toward Wentworth. The girl was retreating, balancing the axe before her as he had. But her eye would be unequal to the task of guarding, her arms feeble in the attack. If only, Wentworth's soul cried, if only he had some weapon *now!* Then his eye caught the wobbling spear in the beast-thing's back.

He bounded forward. Both hands were thrust out before him. His body leaned far forward like that of a man who approaches a dive. Ten feet from the broad, powerful back of the beast-man he launched himself in the air in a long, furious leap. He went in like a tackler, but he aimed much higher, at the broad blunt end of the spear. His hands caught it in midair. He cushioned the butt, brought both hands back against his shoulder in a single movement. His fists made a pad and his shoulder rammed hard against the butt with all the weight of his body, with, behind it, all the force of his headlong dive.

His body stopped dead. His hands and shoulders went numb as if hit by an elephant and he dropped to the earth on hands and knees. For a long moment he crouched there, utterly unable to move. If he had failed....

Finally he staggered to his feet, reeled back two quick paces. He saw the beast man groveling on its face, the spear embedded almost halfway through its back. Over the beast stood the slim straight body of the girl. The axe was lifted high in the air and even as Wentworth regained his feet, the weapon swung down. The aim was true. The girl's body bent like a sapling but the axe bit cleanly through flesh and bone and sinew. The ape man's head rolled from its shoulders. A convulsive, shuddering jerk of the body, then it stiffened, straightened, went limp.

The girl stood straight and trembling. Her hands jerked free of the axe handle, which stuck up at an angle, one edge buried in the earth. Wentworth took a heavy step forward, then a second. The girl stared at him, then jerked up her arms to cover her face. Her shoulders shook with sobs and she stumbled blindly toward him. He put an arm about her and drew her head to his shoulder. Behind him the house collapsed into its foundations with a roaring belch of flame and smoke. A wave of heat washed over them.

CHAPTER 12
THE SHERIFF'S VISIT

WENTWORTH STOOD, half in a daze, patting the shoulder of the crying girl. The other sister crept out of a hedge separating one house from the next and hurried forward. She hesitated in drawing close and Wentworth forced a small smile to his lips. The youngster put an arm about her sister and began to sob, too.

From the darkness of a house across the street, a figure moved. Wentworth narrowed his eyes, steeled himself to further action, but the figure resolved itself soon enough into a stooped old man with a rifle. Wentworth felt anger stir in him. That man had had a rifle and might have helped in the battle.

The old man stopped ten feet away and cackled. "Mad, ain't you, 'cause I didn't take a few shots at yon beast?" He held his rifle at ready.

"It was a coward's role," Wentworth said coldly.

The man shrugged. "They might of come after me if I had." His voice was cracked. "I'll take care of the two girls if you want to do some giant killing, young feller."

Wentworth cursed, and stepped toward him. The rifle came level with his chest.

"Don't start no funny business, young feller."

Wentworth shrugged. "Do you want to go to this man's home?" he asked the girls.

The older girl had cried herself exhausted. She seemed to become aware of her nakedness suddenly, and pressed her sister close as a screen. She looked at the old man.

"Yes," she said wearily, "that'll be all right."

Wentworth nodded. "My name's Richard Wentworth," he told her. "Think you can remember that?" He looked into the girl's eyes and saw that they were a deep quiet gray beneath thin black brows. She nodded gravely.

"You call me up in Horton tomorrow," Wentworth instructed, "and I'll make arrangements to have you taken care of."

The girl nodded once more, eyes set on his. A trembling little smile touched her lips. "I'm 'Lisa Teaford," she said. "I want to thank you for… for…."

Wentworth nodded. "Forget it," he said. "You saved my life a time or two in there, too. Call me tomorrow sure."

He caught the axe from the earth and strode off into the night. Bright red plumes from a dozen fires decorated the sky. Distantly came the crackle of pistol and rifle shots. He moved wearily toward the sounds of battle.

His mind still harked back to the past moments. That girl had been well worth saving. She had courage and loyalty. Nita had fought like that many times, her shoulder to his, her gun barking defiance against his enemies. Wentworth's lips curved in a tired, bitter smile. It was grim that the only tender thoughts he might have of Nita were those of battle, side by side. Grim that they were not thoughts of tender love….

The stutter of a machine gun jerked him up alertly. By God, it would be a wonder if these beasts could stand up against that kind of attack! He broke into a leaden-footed run, the axe swinging at his side.

A barricade had been thrown across the street. The head-lights of automobiles parked beside it threw a vivid glare up the street and now and again a hunched bestial shadow showed itself out in the darkness. When that happened, the machine gun chattered.

As he came closer, a man whirled, with leveled revolver. It was Ron Conley.

"Thank God, you're alive," Conley cried. "A phone call came through from the top of the mountain and we came over, picked up your man Jackson and Beth there…. The phone was only dead in this direction and Jackson managed to fix it up."

Wentworth nodded. That had been prompt and efficient action.

He stared toward the shadows beyond the headlights, where the beasts showed now and again, and suddenly he stiffened. Through a freak of lighting, the glare of a headlight reflected from a window into the darkness between two houses a hundred feet in front of the barricade. And a man was there, a man with a leveled rifle. He snatched Conley's revolver, but before he could snap a shot, the man had vanished. Wentworth cursed under his breath. That man who had aimed a shot behind the barricades, at the defenders of the town, was Jack Hawks—the man the Headsman had pretended to kill!

THE ATTACK of the beast-men gradually dwindled away. The casualties were frightful. Only two of the creatures besides those Wentworth had encountered—had been killed, but twelve houses had been set afire and their occupants murdered or carried away. A half dozen men on guard about the city had been slain, pierced through with spears or battered into shapelessness by sledges.

In several cases, the flames had broken from control and swept over other homes before they had burned themselves out. Few of the occupants had managed to escape. Some preferred to kill themselves in their blazing homes rather than go meet the frightfulness outside.

The tale of casualties stirred Wentworth to fierce anger and the sight of Hawks with the killers was confirmation of his suppositions concerning the human agency behind the hordes, also of his belief that the Headsman had deliberately faked Hawks' murder.

But Hawks, too, was no more than an underling. He could profit from the looting of rich trains and from bank robberies, but the industrial aspects of the horde's operations certainly would net him no profit. In his weary mind, Wentworth reviewed the list of those who could benefit from the Headsman murders, and from those killings on the West Coast. This man, Taliaferro, of course, might well find the death of gold mine owners useful. Taliaferro and Welver together—it was not necessarily true that Welver had been kidnapped—might have some gigantic plan.

Wentworth pressed his throbbing temples with his palms. He recalled suddenly that the man who had financed Hawks' last trip was Oscar Hedley, who had been sufficiently prominent in gold share dealings…. By heavens, the Spider had overlooked a bet there. Perhaps he had been foolish, too, not to check up more closely on Tremaine James. Certainly James as well had a finger in many industrial pies…. But damn it, a clever man certainly would have done nothing so obvious as be present at the time of Glastonbury's offensive speech, if he had any hostile intent.

Now Wentworth lay back, relaxed, in the rear of a car which Jackson drove over the brightening roads toward Horton. He was returning alone, leaving Beth Welver to follow with Conley. He had forced her to give up her position with the railroad— there would be no further information *that* way for a while, he told himself grimly.

In Horton, he sped directly to the hotel. There on his way to summon Nita, he glimpsed her in the dining room with a man. The man, he saw, was Ted Masters. The explorer sprang to his feet and swung about the table to greet him, pumping his hand enthusiastically. He looked neat and fresh beside Wentworth's battered appearance. Wentworth had washed and put on fresh clothing in Coonville, but his face was scarred from the battle, drawn with fatigue.

Masters' red beard seemed fairly to jiggle with animation. "Wish I could have been in on that fight last night," he boomed.

"Just my luck to be off in the hills and return too late to accomplish anything. They tell me you covered yourself with glory."

Wentworth made a wry face. "Some might call it glory. I had some trouble washing it off."

Nita laughed. Her hand was on her beloved's arm, and now he looked down at her gravely, a slow smile lifting the corners of his mouth. Her face was so fresh, her violet eyes so bright. He pressed her hand against his side, but said nothing of what shone in his gaze.

"Glory's so useless he washes it off!" she cried, and laughed again, deep in her throat.

WENTWORTH SAT down to breakfast and Masters began a circumstantial account of his search for the tribe of beast-men. He had found one bivouac, he reported: a series of filthy caves in a mountainside. But apparently they had been abandoned days before. When the creatures moved through the hills they left almost no trail. "I surprised one of the things hunting," Masters said, "and he damned near finished me before he realized he was dead."

Wentworth nodded, smiling a little. His eyes studied the other's keenly alive face, the lean, hard line of jaw beneath the curly red beard, the flashing eyes. An extraordinarily vital man.

"I'll tell you about my fight some time," he remarked. "But it would make rather gory table talk. My guns were empty when I tackled the last one."

He turned toward Nita. "Darling, there's a girl over in Coonville who had the narrowest possible escape from death and lost her father and mother…" he told briefly of the fight. "I think you'd better take her under your wing for a while, beautiful."

Nita nodded easily. Masters had fallen quiet, tracing idle designs on the tablecloth.

"This business has played hell with my writing," he said slowly. "I had only a couple of chapters written when I spotted the first of those beasts and since then…" He shrugged.

There was a sudden heavy trampling in the hall. Three men started past the door, halloo-ing for the proprietor, saw the group in the dining room, and stalked forward.

"You're Wentworth, ain't you?" the leader demanded. Seeing the bulge of a gun beneath the man's left arm, catching a glint of an official star badge, Wentworth frowned. His quick eyes took in the two behind the leader and saw that they also were armed. He stood up.

"My name is Wentworth," he said quietly. "What do you want?"

The leader, a lean, gangly mountain man, with shrewd eyes above high cheekbones, shoved his hat to the back of his head.

"I'm sheriff of these parts, and I got a warrant for your arrest," he said. "Come from New York. 'Pears like you're wanted for a murder up there."

He spoke slowly, shifting a wad of chewing tobacco from cheek to cheek. But there was tension in his body and his right hand clung to one lapel, close to his under-shoulder gun.

"I hope you ain't goin' to make no trouble," he drawled.

Kirkpatrick's warning flashed through Wentworth's mind. The advice to return to New York. He had ignored it to remain here and battle against the destructive hordes of beast-men. This was the answer.

He measured the sheriff and his two deputies, eyes sharp behind the mask of his smile. He could best them all right, pretend to go calmly toward the sheriff, hold out his hands as though for shackles, then grab the man and use him as a shield. It would not be the first time he had battled for humanity while all mankind hunted him on charges of murder.

"I'm not inclined to make trouble," he said calmly, "but I'd like to hear your warrant."

He was conscious of Nita's eyes upon him. He saw that she had drawn her feet beneath her, ready to throw herself between the officers and himself should he wish to attempt an escape. Masters was looking from accused to accuser, his face twisted in amazement. He got to his feet.

"Look here," he said, "there must be some mistake. This is the chap who fought the beast-men in Coonville last night. He saved those two girls from being carried off...."

The sheriff got rid of several ounces of tobacco juice out a window. "Yeah, I know. But the warrant came through and I gotta serve it."

Wentworth knew suddenly that he was not going to attempt to escape, that he was going back to New York to face trial. Jackson and Ram Singh, under Nita, could follow up the clue about Hawks. Perhaps in the trial he would be able to gain some further clue to the brain behind all this crime. When he had beaten the murder frame-up....

The sheriff had drawn out the warrant and was reading it weightily, rolling the words off his tongue.

Wentworth nodded. "All right, Sheriff, I'll go with you."

Nita's eyes were intently on his face. He smiled down at her. "I'll waive extradition and you can wire Commissioner Flynn to send for me at once." He was talking to the sheriff, but his eyes never left Nita's. He leaned over abruptly and kissed her.

"Good bye, darling."

CHAPTER 13
ON TRIAL FOR LIFE

THROUGH THE first days of his trial, Wentworth was inclined to smile at the evidence. It was, to him, such a patent frame-up. Then he realized that none of the jurors would look at him and that was bad. For another thing, the prosecutor had cannily insisted on selecting a jury from the poorer people, the natural enemies of men of wealth. They were eager to believe evil of him.

Even when Wentworth saw the trend however he could not believe that the jury would decide against him. But despite his own certainty of innocence, the defense seemed weak to him. His charges of frame-up by the Headsman, whom he had been fighting, were unconvincing even when supported by stories of his conquest over Underworld characters, the few he had conquered in his own identity. And he could give no alibi without admitting that he was the Spider.

For two days, the defense wrangled and worried at the case

against him. A procession of incredibly prominent character witnesses took the stand, though Wentworth would not permit Governor Kirkpatrick to be called. He was not going to permit Kirk to be involved…. But Kirkpatrick came voluntarily, saying that his good friend Wentworth had refused to use the governor's prestige, but he wished to testify.

Kirkpatrick dropped a hand on his shoulder as he left the witness stand, but Wentworth read doubt in his friend's keen eyes, in the rigidity of his gaunt strong face. Kirkpatrick had just left when Nita entered the court, snubbing attendants who would have stopped her, and made her way forward to sit at the counsel table, a few feet away.

It was not until Nita came, not until he saw the defiant cast of her smile, that Wentworth understood. Nita had come because she believed he would be convicted. It must be so. If she had not thought he would need her, she would never have left her task. Kirkpatrick has been the last defense witness. The lawyers were arguing before the jury now and Wentworth leaned across table to smile into Nita's eyes.

"Thanks, beautiful," he formed the words soundlessly with his lips.

NITA VAN SLOAN

Nita rose in her chair, leaned across the table while a police guard started suddenly to his feet to interfere, and kissed Wentworth on the lips. Then she sat back smiling a little, her cheeks flushed, but with her head set at a proud angle. There was a ripple of whispering among the spectators and the judge's gavel slapped the desk. Newspaper men scooted for the doors.

Wentworth's lips twisted. He looked down at his hands, clasped loosely in his lap. The lawyer's words reached him in a slow, portentous drone.

"There can be no doubt in any honest man's mind but that this man, Wentworth, with his ridiculous notions of offended honor, went to the home of the honorable former district attorney, Robert Glastonbury, and deliberately provoked him into a quarrel in which Glastonbury stood no chance at all. He shot Glastonbury through the heart before that mighty man of peace could even lift his weapon...."

Wentworth's disgust exploded in a snort of scarcely suppressed mirth. Mighty man of peace! Such flamboyancy as this was part and parcel of the law which had driven him to become the Spider, wasn't it? The law which often protected the guilty and sent the innocent to prison because of the ambitions of the prosecutors.

HE KNEW suddenly what the verdict of that jury would be. And with the thought his eyes skimmed over the court room with a bright, hard calculation.

This room was on the third floor of the building, so the windows offered no escape. The door was guarded by two men inside, two outside, and there were four police beside him constantly.

True, he had fought greater odds, but the crowd thronging the benches was an added menace. They would get in his way. Some of them might be wounded, killed. The light in his eyes became ugly and sardonic. Let them be killed! What did the Spider care now for the humanity he defended?

Humanity had turned on him, hadn't it? It had thrown him here into this dock before the bar which was, very legally, forcing him toward the electric chair and death. But even while he mocked himself in this way, he knew he would not make the attempt, would not risk the lives of these hostile spectators to free himself. It was not for the individual member of society that he fought, though he could wage mighty warfare for them, too; it was for his ideal of justice and right.

Justice and right! This court typified such things, didn't it? And this court was sending him to his death?

His eyes, desperate and bitter, swung to Nita. They looked at each other and while they looked, the courtroom seemed to fade away and leave them standing, alone and unafraid, upon the brink of a precipice. Wentworth realized sharply that if he made the plunge, Nita would go with him.

"No," he said, "No, no!" He rose to his feet shouting. "No!"

Nita was still smiling quietly into his face. The judge slammed his gravel on the rostrum; lawyers whirled to stare at him. Wentworth recovered himself with an effort which tensed his whole body. His lips twisted in a smile, and the madness went from him. He bowed suavely to the judge.

"I humbly crave your pardon, Your Honor." His voice was clear and mocking. "I must have forgotten myself."

He sat down and for a while longer there was absolute silence in the room. The judge made a gruff reprimand and turned to the jury, continuing his charge.

"You must find either a verdict for first degree murder or you must acquit this man. The law does not recognize the code of the duel, but even if it did, this man was palpably the aggressor since the crime was committed in the home of Robert Glastonbury. It was a combat in which the aggressor ran no risk whatever, since the victim knew nothing of firearms…. If you believe the evidence that this is the man who entered Glastonbury's home that night…."

The judge's voice droned on. Wentworth lost the words again, staring into Nita's eyes. He turned away finally, looking blankly into nothingness. He tried to think of the reasons behind his presence here, the crimes of the Headsman and his Neanderthal hordes, the cleverness of the man who had framed such inescapable evidence. Now he realized that he had made the mistake of all men who live constantly in the face of peril. Ultimately he had underestimated the peril—in this case the strength of the case against him. He should have remained free at all costs, and sought proof of his innocence. He had preferred the course which led to the defense of humanity, rather than of himself.

He stirred as the jurors arose and in single file marched through a high, heavy door. The door was closed behind them and the court adjourned. When it was called again, it would be to hear the foreman of the jury say….

Wentworth felt himself pulled to his feet, felt the cold steel of a handcuff fastened to each wrist. From between his guards he looked at Nita. She smiled, and slowly his head came up. He smiled, too, and the policeman led him away to his cell. He was sleeping soundly when, hours later, an officer rattled the gate to arouse him.

"Come on. Snap out of it! Them jurors've made up their mind."

He made his toilet swiftly but perfectly and then submitted with good grace to the handcuffs. The courtroom was more

136

crowded than ever. Nita sat as before, at the counsel table, greeting him with a gay smile. They all stood while the judge came in. Wentworth's smile was mocking. Make way for the majesty of the law!

He sat very straight while the jury filed in and the judge's grave deep voice asked if they had arrived at their decision. The foreman's words were clipped. They seemed a little angry.

"Yes, Your Honor, we have."

"Defendant, rise and face the jury. Jury, face the defendant. Gentlemen, what is your verdict?"

Wentworth's smile, as he faced the jury, was nonchalant, even debonair. His eyes were bright and questioning.

"We, the jury, find the defendant guilty, as charged, of first degree murder."

A HEAVY rock seemed to strike Wentworth in the pit of the stomach. He heard Nita draw in a deep, quavering breath. But he did not alter his facial expression. He achieved a small, graceful bow in the direction of the jury.

"Thank you, gentlemen," he said clearly. He faced the judge. "Get on with the show, Pilate."

The judge's heavy, dewlapped face quivered a little with anger. He spluttered as he demanded, "Has the defendant anything to say before I sentence him?"

Wentworth appeared to weigh that question gravely. He sighed. "I can't think of anything really brilliant," he said, "So I'd best—what do you call it—stand mute?"

The judge put on a black cap and Wentworth feigned polite attention. It required all his fortitude to put on this show. But he had to do it. His own personal peace of mind demanded fortitude.

"The defendant left the courtroom a broken man." No, the news men would not write that of him. They would not. He smiled even when the judge pronounced sentence of death.

"I beg your pardon," he said. "What was that date? I wouldn't want to forget the engagement."

Laughter rippled over the spectators. Nita smiled on him tenderly. She knew what a struggle went on within him. She knew how he fought for these last few moments of courage.

The judge slammed the gavel down violently on the bench.

"I see no reason for facetiousness, young man," he said heavily. "Do you realize that I am sentencing you to die?"

"Quite," Wentworth spoke cheerfully. "That was why I wanted to make sure of the date."

The judge was beyond anger now. He leaned back, regarding the condemned man with a preternaturally grave face. He shook his head heavily.

"The date is the week of August 10," he said clearly. "Take the prisoner away."

CHAPTER 14
NITA TAKES COMMAND

NITA WANTED with all her being to throw herself into Wentworth's arms the moment the judge ceased speaking. That moment when all the courtroom was still. This was the end, the end of the trial. She fought against a thought that this was the end, too, of everything for her and Dick Went-worth. She did not throw herself into his arms.

Instead she turned toward him and waved a jaunty hand. "I'll be seeing you, Dick," she said, and grinned impishly at her own slang.

It was the bracer Wentworth needed. He jerked his head in a cheerful nod. "The address is Sing Sing," he replied. "I don't believe I know the telephone number."

The two cops on either side grinned admiringly and their voices were pleasant when they urged him toward the Bridge of Sighs. He did not look back.

Nita stood rigidly, a stiff smile on her lips, as long as he was in sight. She wanted to cry, to scream and shout his innocence. But it would do no good. It would be a silly display.

Behind her she heard the judge. "A more remarkable display of sheer nerve, I never saw," he said. "You'd best guard him well. Such bravado must have its basis in a certainty of escape."

Nita dropped her eyes at last, slowly drew on her gay knitted gloves. Fools! They should know that Dick's courage had sprung rather from the certainty of death. He had no hope of escape—escape from the death house of Sing Sing? It was ridiculous on the face of it. The death house was an armed fortress within a double defense of prison house and high walls. Rifle guards paced those walls and in the lookout towers at the corners were machine guns....

She was frowning down at her gloves, uselessly smoothing out each finger. If all other things failed, she would try that escape, but that would be a last desperate hope. There must, there

In the face of machine gun fire, Jackson clashed toward the wrecked car.

must be a way of finding the murderer of Glastonbury. Once let her find the man—her lips tightened in an unconscious imitation of the Spider's smile—once let her find the guilty man and he would talk. God, yes, he would talk!

Her head came up, and the smile on her lips became pleasant. A girl reporter, sob sister for a newspaper, edged close. "Oh, it's too terrible, Miss van Sloan. Too terrible. What will you do now?"

Nita smiled sweetly at her. "Shave off my hair and enter a nunnery for murderer's sweethearts," she said clearly.

The girl reporter's eyes narrowed and her over-red lips hardened. "That'll make a swell story," she said. "Don't you want to say something else?"

"I am also," said Nita, moving off, "going to take an oath of silence."

Nita did not dodge, but neither would she pose, for the newspaper photographers who thronged the steps of the courthouse. She wore her smile for them all, and she was still smiling as she entered Wentworth's Lancia with Ram Singh rigid at the door.

When the crowds were left behind, however, the starch went out of her and she slumped down in the seat feeling very tired, very small, very weak. If the Spider had failed to run to earth the Headsman, how could *she* hope to?

SHE HAD a month and three days to find the real murderer. And she threw herself violently into the task. She made no pretense of finding or conquering the Headsman. All she wanted was the underling who had actually slain Glastonbury. She made certain arrangements with Ram Singh. Once let her settle upon a suspect, and they would learn the truth or....

An hour after the verdict was returned, before Wentworth had ever been started on his heavily guarded way to the Sing Sing death house, she had Jackson and Ram Singh in her apartment high up in the Riverside Towers. From the broad studio windows she could look down on the sun-beaten waters of the Hudson, but she stared blindly today, feeling the waiting tension in herself, in Jackson, and in Ram Singh.

These two would be faithful to the death, she knew, but they would miss the Spider's guiding hand. *Her* brain must guide them now. *She* must be the one who led their battling footsteps. And the stake—the stake was Dick Wentworth's life!

She steeled herself. Her face was white, drawn, but full of hard purpose as she turned from the window.

Both men stood stiffly at attention, Jackson in the army manner, eyes staring straight ahead, Ram Singh imperturbable behind folded arms, his turbaned head at a defiant angle. Smoldering fires lay in the eyes of both men.

"I'm not going to let them murder Dick," she said. Her voice surprised even herself with its taut, hard rasp. The music seemed stripped from it. It was as if she spoke no longer with her own tongue, but with that of the Spider. Jackson and Ram Singh stiffened. Surprise touched their faces, too—surprise and determination.

"This isn't melodramatics," she went on. "But I won't permit it, if we have to blow up Sing Sing to prevent it. I've made certain arrangements with Professor Brownlee in case everything else fails. But that's a desperate chance, a last resort which may fail.

"Does either of you know a man who serves the Headsman? This must not be suspicion. It must be fact."

Jackson slowly shook his head. Ram Singh muttered a negative.

Nita's face went even paler. Her violet eyes seemed to burn in deep sockets, for dark smudges ringed her eyes.

"Then this is what we must do," she said, her voice metallic "We must select a known criminal, one known to be a murderer, and we must—" she hesitated, steeled herself with clenched hands—"we must kill that criminal and put the Spider's seal upon his forehead. When we've done that, the Headsman will reveal himself in some way. He knows Dick is the Spider. He knows we're his friends, and he'll see that we intend to carry on. He will try to eliminate us."

Jackson's eyes fixed on her face with something like awe, and slowly his hard-jawed face relaxed to a grin. Ram Singh's eyes were burning.

Nita drew a deep breath. "When the Headsman renews the attack, it will be up to you two to capture one of his men. Ram Singh will see that he talks, that he confesses the name of the man who killed Glastonbury."

Jackson's grin became set. He said, under his breath, "By God!"

NITA FELT that she was no longer herself. Some other power had taken control of her. There was no compassion in her heart, no room for anything except bitter determination and hatred. Her red lips curved in a smile that was strange on her white, tension-thinned face.

"Don't you like my plan, Jackson?" she asked silkily.

He said flatly, "It should achieve results."

"Don't you like my plan, Jackson?"

Jackson quivered. He dropped on one knee and took her hand between his. "Miss Nita," his voice rasped, "on my knees, I renew my pledge. I serve you and the major to the death. I did not hesitate. It is only that I did not know… I did not know you could… think such things."

"As torturing a criminal to save Dick?" she asked quietly. She laughed suddenly, and her laughter was harsh and thin. "I would kill a dozen men, and you and me, too, to save him."

For a moment silence throbbed in the room. Ram Singh also dropped on one knee and bowed his head with his hands to his forehead.

"So be it," he murmured. "To the death!"

Nita calmed herself with a violent effort. "I think," she said quietly, "that we'll save him. I've already chosen the man who is to die. Bart Schmidt. He killed that child who was kidnapped a month ago. Politics got him off...."

Jackson drew a deep breath. Got slowly to his feet. "That shall be my job," he said heavily. "Will you give me the Spider's seal?"

She took Wentworth's cigarette lighter from her corsage and held it out. "The base comes off. Press the bottom of the lighter to Schmidt's forehead... afterward."

Jackson saluted, about-faced, and strode from the apartment.

Ram Singh got stiffly to his feet, and stood against the wall with folded arms. He knew his task came later.

Nita walked slowly back to the window. Many of the small panes were open and warm air streamed in. She dragged a hand across her forehead, disarranging her curls. Her eyes were fixed on the skies. She closed them, her face lifted. She stood like that for a long time.

IT WAS after four o'clock when the doorbell buzzed faintly. Nita lay asleep on the cushions before the window and Ram Singh had gently covered her with blankets. She started up at the sound of the bell. Ram Singh strode on silent swift feet down the short hallway. Nita was conscious that the sky was very black, and that no traffic sounds arose from Riverside Drive below.

The door let in a widening bar of light and she recognized Jackson's wide-shouldered silhouette as he strode forward. She saw that his left arm was held stiffly, the hand in the pocket. Ram Singh touched up soft lights and she got rigidly to her feet. Jackson held the glittering cigarette lighter out to her, a tight, hard smile on his lips. Nita saw that there was an ugly red stain on his left sleeve.

She accepted the lighter with a lifting heart. "Good work, Jackson," she said quietly. "Ram Singh, get his coat off. I'll take care of that wound."

She found unknown reservoirs of strength within her. The feeling of command, the heady knowledge that men accepted her orders, she found good. In the morning the newspapers told her how Bart Schmidt had died. In the midst of a roistering party at a cabaret a black-cloaked figure had appeared and taxed Schmidt with the kidnapping murder. The shooting had been swift and deadly. Schmidt and his bodyguard had died, two women had fled, and police, rushing to the scene, had found both gangsters with the seal of the Spider on their foreheads.

But Nita made no further comment to Jackson on the efficiency of his work. She knew that he wanted none. He was serving a master whom he loved, and the success of his mission was its own reward.

Under her guidance, the three of them set up a regular regime of living which included, each afternoon at dusk, a drive through

Policemen were firing ineffectually at the diving plane.

Central Park. For, Nita explained, they must make it easy for the Headsman to learn their habits and plan his attack.

Four days elapsed. Jackson's flesh wound was already healing nicely when they received the first intimation that they were being followed. A dilapidated black coupé had appeared in their wake for the second day in succession.

The next afternoon Nita paced her apartment nervously. From coffee table to mantel, to the table against the wall, moving little ornaments, adjusting a picture on the wall, rearranging the implements beside the fire place. She was eager for the ride at dusk....

Finally she was facing her two stalwart men with a tight little smile.

"You must not kill them all," she said. "One must be taken prisoner and... turned over to Ram Singh."

Ram Singh's hand strayed to the long knife hidden in his sash. His knuckles whitened as he clasped it.

"By Siva!" he whispered. "By Siva!"

The Lancia was bulletproof in both its glass and its heavy doors. In it Jackson and Ram Singh sat rigidly erect on the front seat, while she herself lounged behind beside her Great Dane, Apollo, whom she had brought back from a boarding farm this very day. The huge dog seemed to sense the excitement; kept his paws on the back of the front seat, his massive, intelligent head peering forward intently. The windows of the Lancia were all open but the touch of an electric button would shut them all.

The dilapidated coupé which had followed them on two previous days was stationed near the entrance of the park today.

As the Lancia passed, its horn sounded three times in quick succession and Nita's lips smiled. She kept her hand on the button which would close the windows.

In a rear vision mirror, attached in the tonneau, she watched for an attacking car which she was sure would soon make its appearance. Traffic on the east drive of the park was thick, homeward bound. That would simplify matters for the gunmen who would come presently. It would be simple to crash their way through the traffic. The confusion following would effectually block pursuit.

THE TRAILING car identified itself first by the fact that it contained four men. A heavy powerful sedan. After watching it for a full minute, while the stream of traffic flowed northward through the deepening dusk, Nita caught up the speaking tube and warned Ram Singh in a sharply elated voice.

"I'll close the windows when they get close," she said. "I'll leave the course of action to you two. One of them must live!"

Apollo turned his head and looked at her with eyes that seemed to understand what portended. He growled deep in his chest Nita's smile was wintry. Beneath her right hand lay a .38 automatic Wentworth had given her. Her left hand rested on the button which would close the car windows. She watched the heavy sedan crawl up from the rear.

When the nose of it crept past her window, she pressed the button and the bulletproof windows zipped up from their sockets. She opened a central port in the one nearest and laid her gun barrel in the slot. She glanced once at Jackson and Ram Singh. The ex-sergeant held an automatic in his hand and was watching the sedan with narrowed eyes. He made no move to fire yet. Ram Singh was more active. He was pulling the steering wheel slowly to the left, crowding the gangsters' car.

Nita smiled once more and turned back to her gun port. She saw that the gangster to the right had a sub-machine gun cradled in his lap. His window was open all the way. At sight of Nita, he lifted the weapon and began shooting.

Nita shrank aside. She fired slowly, deliberately, as Wentworth had taught her. She had fired three times before the machine gunner reached a spot directly opposite the window. The glass before her was frosted over by the impact of the bullets, but the gangster's gun stopped firing. Peering through the port, she saw him slump forward over his weapon.

She saw, too, that other cars had cleared a path for them, and that Ram Singh, hands steady on the delicate steering apparatus, was crowding the other machine closer and closer to the narrow strip of grass separating the road from the thick trees in the park. Jackson spilled over the back of the seat and crouched on the floor at her feet, opening another gun port. In each hand he held a heavy Colt .45, and with these he kept up a deliberate, careful fire.

The driver of the gang car seemed only now to realize that his mates were getting the worst of the battle, and he tried to spurt ahead, out of the slowly narrowing hole into which Ram Singh was crowding him. The Lancia kept easy pace, edging a little ahead, jamming in even closer. One of the pair in the back of the other car was down and now the second man, his face white and frightened, fumbled with the catch of the door on the far side.

"Shoot the driver," Nita said calmly," and put a bullet through the other man's leg. The driver isn't apt to know so much."

Jackson nodded, his lips stiffening into a grin. He fired three times rapidly and the sedan veered wildly, side-swiped the Lancia, then swung in the opposite direction, nose on into the trees. It hit one with a rending crash, bounced aside, and rolled five feet farther before it slithered to a halt.

Ram Singh braked instantly, holding the Lancia steady. They stopped within ten feet and Jackson was out even before, running in great leaping bounds toward the wrecked car. A gun stabbed orange flame at him but he only zig-zagged madly. Once more the gun crashed and Nita, aiming high, emptied her own that way in a swift roll of fire.

That did it. The one remaining gunman flung from the far side of the sedan and sprinted for the woods. Jackson rounded the rear of the car at the same instant and launched into a flying tackle. Both went down in a huddle, but Jackson was up instantly. He reached low and struck once, then jerked the unconscious gunman to his shoulder and came toward the Lancia in a steady, jogging trot.

Distantly a police siren shrilled, and passenger cars, streaming in endless lines past the scene of battle, eddied excitedly. A few swerved to the side of the road and men ran toward Jackson. He blasted two shots over their heads. One man flung flat, another turned and fled shrieking toward his own car. Jackson shouldered his burden into the tonneau. With Apollo growling and showing his teeth at the unconscious gangster, Ram Singh got under way instantly.

An excited taxi driver followed them for a dozen blocks but Ram Singh lost him soon enough. He dropped Nita at her doorway. Jackson alighted stiffly, too. Nita's quick eyes saw that his wound had broken open again and was staining his tunic. He hid that by carrying a lap robe and they went immediately to her apartment. Then, his wound recared for, Jackson stood guard at the doorway.

TWO HOURS later, a police sergeant blustered into the apartment. He was truculent in manner, but Nita's cool hauteur soon reduced him to humbleness. She got Commissioner Flynn by telephone while the policeman waited. After that there was no further trouble.

The morning was half over when Ram Singh reported to her. His face was cut by deep lines, his eyes looked hot in dark sockets. But he bowed gracefully, cupping hands to his forehead.

"You have... succeeded?" She faltered over the words. So much depended on the answer. Almost a week of their month had been used in setting this trap. If they had to begin all over again....

Ram Singh bowed, pride glittering in his eyes. *"Han, missie sahib!"*

Her hands gripped together tightly. She fought for calmness. Ram Singh had merely said "Yes," but that little word meant he knew the name of the man who had killed Glastonbury, knew the secret which would free Wentworth.

She moved one hand in a small, awkward gesture, signaling Ram Singh to proceed. "The man who killed *Sahib* Glastonbury," said the Hindu, "was Monk Kurlew. He is now in Paris. I have his address."

Nita stood staring. She knew the man's name, but that alone meant little. "This man you questioned…" Ram Singh bowed, his eyes like glittering bits of jet. "Unfortunately, *missie sahib*, he died."

His voice was expressionless, yet she swayed. There was a hard violence in the very coolness with which the Hindu spoke. Jackson's own eyes were fixed narrowly on that dark, impassive countenance.

Nita drew in a deep, slow breath. "It would have been better if he had lived," she said quietly. "But that cannot be helped."

"He was stubborn," Ram Singh said softly.

Once more the tone struck through her. An involuntary shudder made her tremble. She knew suddenly that she was not built for this type of battle. The stench of men's deeds was hateful in her nostrils. But Ram Singh had acted on her orders. It was her hand that had… had tortured a man to death.

She looked down at her small white hands, their tapered sensuous fingers. A slow, tired smile came to her lips. Well, if it would save Dick, she would bathe those hands in blood! The man who had died had attempted to kill her and her two friends. She steeled herself afresh. Finally she addressed the Hindu.

"Ram Singh, you still have your passport. Go to Paris and bring me back this Monk Kurlew. He must talk. But he must live, too—to be electrocuted for murder."

Jackson started forward, a hand raised in protest. She smiled at him. "There's work here for you, Jackson. We must accumulate the evidence to support this man's confession. We must have the stage entirely set when… Ram Singh returns."

Ram Singh's chest swelled with pride. "Monk Kurlew alive," he said, his words sibilant. *"Han, missie sahib!"* He backed, salaaming, toward the door.

"Remember, Ram Singh," Nita's voice was a tocsin, high and stirring. "Remember, your master's life depends on you."

The Hindu drew himself up. "I shall remember." He salaamed again and was gone.

Nita sank upon a window seat, and presently Apollo came and laid his massive head in her lap. His great brown eyes stared up into hers. Her white hand upon his crown seemed so tiny!

Jackson came forward three paces. "Miss Nita."

The face lifted to him, he saw suddenly, looked old and very tired.

"Yes, I know, Jackson, but we must have another string to our bow. If Ram Singh fails…" She paused, gathering strength against the thought of failure. "If Ram Singh fails—you and I must spring Dick Wentworth from the death house."

He stared at her incredulously. Then, slowly, his hard long mouth curved in an admiring grin.

"Miss Nita, if you say so, we'll by God take him away from the whole United States army!"

CHAPTER 15
DISASTER!

NITA MOCKED her own brave words a dozen times in the two weeks that followed. She saw Wentworth in the death house whenever possible and told him, in the presence of cynical guards, that she had learned the name of the man who killed Glastonbury. Wentworth's ebullient spirits lasted as long as Nita was there but when she had left, they died. He was a gaunt, thin-faced man in the prison's shabby garb. He had not given up all hope, but he knew the perils and the dangers, the possible trip-ups.

At the special instance of the district attorney, the court of appeals already had reviewed his case and failed to interfere. Only one appeal remained, that to the governor, and Wentworth refused to let that be made. He could not put such a trial upon his friend, Kirkpatrick. Well he knew that Kirkpatrick would have his own Gethsemane even without an appeal, knowing that he could save the life of the man who was closer to him than his own kin, but knowing, too, that he could not do it and be true to himself. The evidence had been damning.

On the first day of the third and last week before Wentworth was to walk through the little green door of death, a cablegram came from Ram Singh.

ARRIVE WEDNESDAY MORNING CARONIA
WITH GOODS SUCCESSFUL ALL POINTS

Nita read the cable incredulously, almost afraid to believe.

Then she flung herself full length upon the divan and sobs shuddered over her. An hour later, she and Jackson took off from Newark airport in a plane which, within forty minutes, put her down in Albany. She drove swiftly to the governor's mansion. She was kept waiting fifteen minutes, then ushered into the office. Kirkpatrick met her at the door and there was no lightness in his eyes to greet her radiant smile. Jackson entered and stood stiffly against the wall, while Kirkpatrick escorted Nita to a seat and stood before her.

As always he was immaculately dressed, his dark tailored business suit fitting his powerful body perfectly, the usual gardenia showing in his buttonhole. But despite the sharply waxed points of his mustaches, his face seemed flabby. It was worn. Harsh lines cut about his mouth corners and his tired gray eyes were drawn.

"There's no need to ask why you've come," he said slowly, and Nita started at the flatness of his usually vibrant, clipped accent. He turned, and there was a slump to his shoulders too as he walked behind his desk and dropped into a chair. He smiled faintly. "I must hear you."

Nita shook her head. She could not get the smile off her lips. "It's not what you think," she said. "I have new evidence. I know the man who really killed Glastonbury."

Kirkpatrick sat bolt upright, his hands convulsive on his knees. "You what?" It was a cry, the cry of a man who could not believe the thing he wished to hear.

Nita repeated it. "His name is Monk Kurlew," she said rapidly. "One of the Headsman's men confessed and accused Kurlew. I sent Ram Singh to Paris to bring Kurlew back." She tossed the message to the desk.

Kirkpatrick snatched it up, read it over. Nita could see his eyes follow the line and a half of words twice, three times before he looked up again. The yellow paper was quivering in his fingers.

"The man who confessed," he said, his voice strong, deep-timbered. "Who and where is he?"

Nita shook her head. "He's dead."

KIRKPATRICK STARED at her wordlessly. She leaned forward. "But Kurlew himself is on the way back here. Ram Singh's cable means that he has confessed."

Kirkpatrick seemed dazed. Some of the pleasure went out of his face. "You have confirming evidence?" He seemed afraid of that question.

"We have done the best we could," Nita spoke shortly. "Jackson, working without authority, could not accomplish much. We were afraid, too, that the Headsman would learn what we were doing and forestall us. It won't take long, once Ram Singh gets back. When we get Kurlew's story...."

Kirkpatrick said heavily, "I hope not. By heavens, I hope not!" He looked again at the cable, read it over slowly. "I'll be in New York Wednesday, Nita. If you like I'll have police meet Kurlew at quarantine."

She nodded eagerly. "Please, Kirk. If anything should happen now...."

He rose, came across to her. He took both her hands in his as she stood up. "Don't let anything happen, Nita. I tell you if I were forced to let Dick..." His words died. He patted one of her

157

hands, blinked twice rapidly. "I'll be in New York Wednesday," he concluded sharply, and ushered her to the door.

WEDNESDAY MORNING Nita and Jackson were at the Battery waiting amid a squad of police while a city launch sped down the harbor to meet the *Caronia* at quarantine.

Nita could not stand still. She walked about aimlessly, staring now over the sun-dappled water, now back at the towers of Manhattan, behind her. Her heart was singing with hope, but there was a small cold spot of worry in her breast.

"Don't let anything happen," Kirkpatrick had warned. He had begged that for himself as well as for her and Dick. It meant that he would have to have valid evidence before he would act, before he would save Dick. This was Wednesday and tomorrow night at eleven o'clock, Dick, her Dick, was to walk to his death.

She looked up at the sky and, without conscious volition on her part, began praying. Nothing articulate, no words, just a fierce demand that nothing, nothing should happen.

Jackson stood rigidly at the water's edge, staring down toward the *Caronia*. The liner wouldn't be visible from here because of the intervening bulk of Governors Island. But he would see the nose of the police launch as it pushed around the headland there and ploughed the sunny waters toward the Battery.

The minutes strung out interminably. The police guard lounged, not smoking because they were on duty, but laughing and talking. "Lou Gehrig oughta knock out another homer today. Damn Flynn and his orders to wear tunics all summer… those gray shirts now… Geez, my kid walked last night. Three steps. Yeah…."

Nita moved impatiently away. These men were in the midst of healthy normal life. She was in the midst of death. Dear God, don't let anything happen to Kurlew! It can't, God, it can't! She thought *Dick*.

Jackson stood motionless, staring out over the water, narrowed eyes shaded by the green-lined visor of his uniform cap. Nita saw his back take on added stiffness and she ran with quick little steps to his side.

"Jackson! Do you...."

He stretched out a rigid right arm and Nita stood on tiptoes to sight along it. She saw a small green boat with a high pilot's house on its forward deck, a green pennant at its bow, slice the water around the headland.

"That's the boat," he said. His voice choked queerly.

IT WAS at that instant Nita looked, she never knew why, up toward the dazzling blueness of the sky, and saw the plane. A circling dot high against the sky, circling like a vulture. Her eyes fastened, clung to it. But she didn't say anything. Any hour of the day in Manhattan you could look aloft and see a plane somewhere. "This plane doesn't mean anything," she said under her breath.

Jackson's muscles jerked. "What plane?" he asked hoarsely.

She pointed. And as her arm stretched upward, the plane ceased to circle. It viraged, shot downward in a steep dive which leveled its nose toward the green boat ploughing through the cheerful waters of the harbor.

Nita screamed. The cry rose high and thin and terrible in the sunlight, and a lieutenant of police pounded across the wooden dock to her side.

"What? What's the matter!"

"That plane! It's going to attack the boat!"

"Nonsense!" barked the lieutenant. Yet even as he said it, there was the distant hammer of a machine gun.

The police boat changed its course, veering sharply. Broadside to the watchers on the land now, it made a fast zig-zag toward the cover of Governor's Island.

"They'll never make it!" Jackson groaned.

"They must!" Nita cried. *"They must!"*

The plane was not more than five hundred feet above the water now. Its machine gun hammered again and little jets of white foam spat upward from the surface of the water. A man with a turban stood up straight in the boat, caught another man up in his arms like a baby, and started for the cover of the pilot house. He was halfway there when he stumbled and went down.

Policemen in the boat were crouching, firing ineffective revolvers up at the plane. Nearer and nearer it dived—now three hundred feet from the water, now two hundred. And always the machine gun hammered and hammered. Nita did not know that she was tearing her cheeks with her fingernails, did not know that one hand was gripping the police lieutenant's wrist until her nails dug into his flesh.

She saw the crouching policemen wilt in the boat, saw two tumble overboard into the bullet-churned waters. When the plane finally leveled off at seventy-five feet and bored upward into the blue, not a man was left standing on the launch and it was racing, with wide-open motors, in a great aimless circle. Not even the roof of the pilot house had stood against that rain of lead.

Nita stood there, motionless on the edge of the dock in the sun, until another launch had gone out to the boat and brought it in, until she had seen Kurlew dead on the floor boards of the boat and Ram Singh's bloody but still faintly breathing body rushed off to the hospital. Then she turned and looked at Jackson.

"If only Ram Singh had jumped overboard with him," she said, in a tight, strained voice. She slumped down on the thick boards of the dock in a dead faint.

CHAPTER 16
THE LAST APPEAL

NITA FOUGHT back to consciousness with a sense of insupportable weight upon her chest. An ambulance doctor bent over her with frowning face.

"You must take it easy," he said. "Your heart isn't responding as I'd like to see it."

Was that the weight on her chest? No. There was something else. When the memory stabbed through her she pushed up against his protesting hands. She shook her head doggedly, not even hearing the intern's words.

"Jackson," she called. "Jackson!"

He shoved forward and she gripped his arm. "Kirkpatrick," she said, suddenly weak. "Kirkpatrick at once."

Jackson took her out to the Lancia and moments later they were whirling through the thick, depressing heat of downtown Manhattan, headed for the governor's Pelham Manor home. He had an office there....

Nita lay back on the cushions with her mind almost blank. Whenever her eyes closed, she saw that plane diving down out of an incredibly blue sky, and then the welter in the boat when it had docked. She did not close her eyes often.

The persistent rush of air against her face revived her body a little, but an unshakable lethargy persisted in her mind. She could only think that she must see Kirkpatrick at once. Kirkpatrick was her only hope. He must help Dick until Ram Singh could talk....

A frantic thought drove her hand to the speaking tube. "Ram Singh," she said slowly, indistinctly, "how badly was he hit?"

She saw Jackson's neck muscles tense and he almost failed to swerve aside in time when a taxi shot out of a side street.

"The truth, Jackson!" Her voice was cold. "I must have the truth!"

Jackson's voice seemed expressionless. "He was hit six times, Miss Nita. Once through the lungs. He lost a lot of blood. Doctor shook his head. But you can't tell. Ram Singh... strong."

Nita took that silently, sitting very erect now in the rear of the car, looking very small in the wide seat, small and white and tired. But her violet eyes were burning. Her one thought was: Then he'll recover consciousness. He'll have a chance to talk.

She tried to shame herself for thinking only of that, now that the loyal Hindu had probably given his life in the service of Wentworth. She could not help it. She had no shame. She had no thought except that perhaps Ram Singh could make a statement, that the statement might be enough. She knew that it would be valueless in courts, but perhaps Kirkpatrick.

She buried her face in her hands, and her shoulders jerked. No sound came from between her clenched fingers. The scratches hurt where her fingernails had bit into her cheek. She liked the pain. For a little while she felt frightened and terribly alone. She, she alone, stood between Dick and… and death. And she had blundered.

Presently her head lifted. Her colorless lips were straight. They twisted a little grimly as she touched them with lipstick before entering Kirkpatrick's house. She had hold of herself again; tight, hard hold. It had to be like that. After insisting that Jackson remain in the car, she climbed alone up the broad stone steps to the entrance beneath the *porte-cochère*.

A butler swung the door wide and she waited in a high dark hall which was very cool. She was a slight, girlish figure in the immensity of the old-fashioned foyer, clad in smart blue linens, her chestnut hair curling out from beneath a jaunty stiff straw. KIRKPATRICK CAME into the hall and she knew at once that he already had heard. Her shoulders wanted to slump, but she held them up bravely, saying nothing while they crossed a broad cool room into Kirkpatrick's book-lined office. He got her a chair and then stood before her, looking down into her pale, distraught face. His own was rigid with anger, his eyes glacial. For a full minute he stood so. Then he turned away, behind his desk, lowered himself slowly into his chair, and laid his hands flat on the blotter with the fingers spread. He did not look at her now.

"Six policemen were killed besides Kurlew," he said heavily. "Five more, and Ram Singh were wounded."

Nita leaned forward, her hands twisting. "Ram Singh will recover consciousness," she said. "He may live."

Kirkpatrick said nothing. He moved the fingers of his right hand slowly together, opened them again. She came to her feet. Sudden fright gripped her by the throat. Why didn't he speak?

"Stanley!" she cried. "Stanley!"

Her feet made no sound on the deep soft rug as she stumbled to the desk. Her right hand readied out to him, with cupped fingers, pleading—a pitiful little gesture.

"Stanley, I said Ram Singh would live… to make a statement."

Kirkpatrick lifted his face. The anger was gone from it now and the lines of his mouth corners were deep and harsh. He turned his hands over, so that the palms lay upward.

"Nita," he said slowly. "You know whatever Ram Singh has to say would bear no weight in a court of law."

"Not in court, no. But with the governor. You don't have to follow court procedure. You…."

It was the expression in his eyes which stopped her. Pity… pity for her. He got up and came around the desk again. But she shrank away, her hands lifted against him.

"No," she said thickly. "No."

He stopped, looking at her from under drawn down brows.

"You've made a brave fight, Nita," he said slowly. "I would have accepted Kurlew's evidence, no matter how flimsy it seemed, no matter how well I knew you'd trumped it up…."

Her strangled little cry did not stop him.

"If you could have given me anything to salve my conscience— I'd have grabbed it. I could have argued myself into submission."

She blazed at him suddenly. "Conscience! *Conscience*, is it— when it's Dick's *life* that's at stake!"

He looked at her stony-eyed, not moving. She gripped his arm then. "And you *can't* believe I faked this new evidence. You can't. Why, that plane alone proves that the Headsman was behind it!"

Kirkpatrick shook his head. "It proves you were very clever even wounding Ram Singh. He must have known what was coming. A brave loyal man."

She tried to shake him. His eyes were wide, acutely imploring. "But, but… You mean you believe that plane…."

"Was yours?" He eyed her intently. "I don't know, Nita. The man you named to me, the man you said confessed to Ram Singh before Ram Singh went to Paris…. Well, that man was tortured to death. When your car was attacked in the park, three men were killed and one of them had thirty-eight caliber bullets in him. The kind you fire… And I know how much you love Dick."

Her hands fell away from his sleeve. She looked at him, and slowly, painfully, her eyes became hard and accusative. "You can't believe those things, Kirkpatrick." Her voice was a whisper. "You can't. If you did, you would have had me arrested. You know Dick didn't kill Glastonbury. Why, you and Dick were like brothers.

You fought sometimes, yes. But you love him and he loves you. I know that. You can't believe things like that about him."

Her eyes held his rigidly, now. She went on. "Dick Wentworth is no common murderer. I was with him that night Glastonbury threw the drink in his face. He laughed about it. Said something about the bitterness of men who are defeated. He didn't get angry about it. Dick never did a petty thing in his life." Her voice broke at last. "Oh, Stanley, for the love of God… use your *heart* for once, instead of your head. The heart that knows Dick Wentworth for the man he is. You can't, can't…."

The words trailed off.

And still Stanley Kirkpatrick's face remained unchanged—except that the graven lines deepened to either side of his straight-lipped mouth. Then the pity grew clearer in his eyes, and she staggered back two slow steps and sank into a chair.

"God," she whispered. "God in heaven…."

SILENCE CAME into the room, a great, waiting silence. Nita saw with a sense of surprise that Kirkpatrick wore, as usual, a gardenia in his lapel. How could he? How could *anything* go on in its normal, customary path when Dick… Her throat closed and her thoughts stopped.

He moved his right hand away from his side, turned the palm forward in a small hopeless gesture.

"Nita," he said. His voice was heavy and slow. "Dick has killed many men. We need not quibble about that. He killed justly, eliminating men who were a menace and a danger to society. But the fact remains that he has killed. That does something to a man's mind. Psychologists will tell you that. A man who has

166

killed once, does it the next time more easily. And Dick has killed many, many times. I don't even know how many murders can be laid to the Spider—men found dead with that mocking little red seal upon their foreheads."

He paused, sucked in a deep breath. "Dick's anger got the better of him this time. He probably was suspicious about Glastonbury picking a quarrel with him. He went there…."

He moved his hand again, the same hopeless little gesture.

Nita was looking at his shoes now. They were highly polished. He even shined his shoes, she thought—and tomorrow his friend would die.

She shook herself. She was being foolish. His man did that, of course—shined his shoes.

Slowly she came to her feet. Her purse, of blue linen like her dress, she held before her. She was conscious of its weight, of the hard metal of the gun within it. The heavy .38 automatic which Dick had given her.

"Stanley," she said slowly. "You know Dick is innocent of this murder. You know he didn't kill Glastonbury, and that it's foolish to think I sacrificed the lives of six policemen, perhaps Ram Singh's too, in any such grandstand play as you suggest."

Kirkpatrick's hands were on the edge of the desk behind him. "It doesn't matter what I think," he reminded her heavily. "Ram Singh's statement could not be recognized. Oh, it's all so useless, Nita."

Her face was frozen, immobile, at last. She had unfastened the catch of her purse. "Very well," she said. "Ram Singh's statement would do no good. We do not need that. But you are Dick

Wentworth's friend. For that reason, Stanley, you will commute his sentence to life imprisonment. Say that you do not believe in capital punishment. It's a fact, anyway, that you do not. Say anything, but save his life...."

Her voice stayed flat, emotionless. It was as if she knew the answer in advance.

The answer came. Kirkpatrick did not even raise his eyes. "Dick would not sanction that plea," he said. "He knows I've warned him, pleaded with him to give up the life he's been living. He knows I shan't falter in my duty."

"Duty?" She was suddenly fierce all over again. "Duty, hell... *It's your damned conceit!*"

Kirkpatrick looked up sharply. The oaths, in her mouth, sounded rough and menacing. Her hand was inside her purse.

He smiled a little, wearily. "I wish it were only conceit, I could...."

He stopped, his lips shutting tightly. He was looking into the black mouth of the automatic. Nita held it expertly. Her hand did not tremble. She held it pointed straight at his heart.

"You will sign a commutation of sentence at once," she said. "If you refuse... I'll shoot you down as I would a dog."

HE WAS as still as a statue, looking at her. He saw the tensity about her mouth, which even the paint of the lipstick could not mask. He saw the same tensity in her gun hand, and the steadiness of her aim. He saw that she would do as she had said—and he laughed.

"Use sense, Nita. Even if I signed such an order, it would

have no force. It would not be honored because I would countermand it."

She took a step forward. "Sign the paper," she said. Her voice was still deliberate, without hysteria. "You are willing to murder Dick. You needn't think I'll hesitate to murder you."

Kirkpatrick's hold on the edge of the desk tightened. He leaned forward from the waist, and his body jerked with the vehemence of his words.

"Shoot then," he said sharply. "Go ahead and shoot! Do you think life is that precious to me? Do you think that I'll care so damned much to live, after... after...." His face seemed to go to pieces before her eyes. His mouth twisted out of shape; after the violence of his speech his body continued to jerk, and tears spilled from his eyes.

"Go on... *shoot!*" he repeated. "Do you think you love Dick more than I do? Do you think a mere woman's love can equal the love of two men...."

His voice broke and his body went lax. His head bowed until the chin pressed against his collar. "God!" he gasped. "You would do me a favor if you'd shoot!"

The gun sagged in her hand. She looked at it curiously, then groped for her bag. She had to fumble twice before she got it inside. She stared down at the rug for an instant, and lifted her head again to watch the bright tears coursing down his face.

"Well," she said wearily. "Well, I guess it isn't conceit."

Turning she moved woodenly toward the door. She had almost reached it when his hand fell on her shoulder. For a moment her old anger surged back, the muscles tensed beneath

169

that touch. But they sagged again. Without glancing around, she waited. His words came to her like that.

"Nita… I've signed four stays of sentence, and three commutations of sentence for Dick—and I've torn up every one of them. If I could pardon him…" His words came strongly all at once. "Nita… I think Dick would tell you this himself… that short of pardon he would prefer the ch… prefer to go at once. He would not even want a stay."

She said nothing. She reached blindly for the doorknob, pulled the heavy door toward her.

"Nita, you understand!" It was a cry.

Nita laughed sharply. She went out through the door and slammed it hard. Understand? What difference, what difference did understanding make—now?

Her feet made little dragging noises on the smooth dark floor of the hall. The butler swung the outer door wide and she stumbled out to where Jackson stood rigidly erect. She did not need to speak. The truth was in every listless, dragging step she took. He helped her into the car.

"Miss Nita," he whispered, "there's still the… other string to our bow!"

Other string—bow? To storm Sing Sing and take Dick from his cell. To smash through the heavily armed outer wall, through the prison building, to that triply guarded fort within a fort: the death house. She laughed again. Tonight, tonight….

CHAPTER 17
THE DEATH WATCH

IN HIS cell in the death house, Wentworth stood motion-less, his hands clasped behind him, and looked at the vacant four-by-six across the narrow hall. Last Thursday night he had seen a man walk out of that door. He hadn't walked far, three paces perhaps, then he stumbled and pitched to the floor in a dead faint. It had delayed the execution perhaps two minutes. Wentworth's mouth twitched.

The guard, seated outside the door, rustled a newspaper and grinned at Wentworth.

"Most fellas put on weight in here," he said amiably, "but I think you done lost some."

Wentworth smiled slightly. "It's quite likely," he said. "You remind me I haven't done my daily calisthenics."

He gripped the bars of the open grill doorway, swung down until he squatted on his heels, straightened again. He did that fifty times without slowing his rhythm. When he finished his breathing was quickened a very little.

"Say, you're in swell shape, buddy," the guard's eyes were admiring.

"Sure," Wentworth's lips quirked again. "Fine shape."

The guard's eyes dropped. It was a *faux pas* for a guard to mention anything that might remind the prisoner what was coming for him. That was a rule of the humanitarian warden of the prison, who was heartily opposed to capital punishment. The guard lifted his eyes again.

"You know," he said, "I hope that girl does get something on this guy for you. Get you a stay anyway. She looked like the goods."

Wentworth said "Thanks," very gravely. He heard the sound of a door opening at the end of the hall opposite, from the green door, and craned his neck, staring that way. He was suddenly hopeful. This was the day Ram Singh was due back from Europe with the man who had killed Glastonbury. He glimpsed the white, heavy face of the warden and his heart quickened. He told himself sharply that he was being foolish. If this were actually a reprieve or a release, he would have been summoned to the warden's office. The warden would not come to him.

He stepped back as the warden stopped outside the door. They nodded pleasantly to each other.

"I have a special order from the governor," the warden said slowly. "It authorizes me to permit you to marry Miss Nita van Sloan here, tomorrow night."

The smile stayed on Wentworth's lips. His heels were flat on the floor, his back rigid. His teeth clicked together. If Nita had made those arrangements, she had been to see Kirkpatrick. That meant....

"What happened?" Wentworth asked thickly. "What happened when the *Caronia* came in?"

The warden's face was emotionless. He had schooled it through years of ceaseless watch in the prison, of watching other men die at his order. His eyes were masked.

"An airplane shot up the police launch on which they were

bringing a man named Monk Kurlew ashore," the warden said slowly. "The plane killed six policemen and Kurlew."

Wentworth's hands closed stiffly into fists. "And my man, Ram Singh?" he asked heavily.

"Five policemen were wounded and two have died since then," the warden went on. "A Hindu whose name I did not catch is in a critical condition at the hospital. They say he tried to shield Kurlew with his body."

The bars of the gate before Wentworth seemed to tilt crazily. The warden's face swelled and receded. Then the pain of his teeth sinking into his lower lip brought Wentworth out of his daze. He shook his head and when he met the warden's gaze again, his eyes were steady and clear, his chin was up.

"Thank you for coming so promptly, warden," he said. "I appreciate your interest."

The warden nodded. "About this wedding?" he said. "You wish it?"

Wentworth bowed. "It would be a great favor. Will you convey my thanks to the governor?"

"Certainly," the warden turned to go. "I shall send the county clerk to you later. You will give him the information for the license." His voice faded down the corridor. Wentworth stood as before, head bowed, hands locked behind him.

"Cheez, buddy, I'm sorry," growled the guard.

WENTWORTH SANK down upon the cot, holding his head between his hands. Until this moment he had hoped. Nita had fought courageously, she and Jackson and brave Ram Singh. But the Headsman had been too much for them. In the back of his mind, had been the hope that even if this main chance failed, perhaps Kirkpatrick's heart would waver at the last moment, that he would break with his stern duty and commute the sentence.

He dropped his hands, staring at the blank steel wall. But he did not want that, no commutation of sentence. Unless the life term would permit him to escape. That was nonsense, of course. Men did not escape from Sing Sing and remain at liberty. And it would be no use in his getting away unless it were soon, unless it would permit him to solve the mystery of Glastonbury's murder and prove his own innocence. The death of Monk Kurlew made that next to impossible. So that....

Resolutely, he thrust such thoughts from his mind. Instead he thought of Nita. He knew that, despite his injunction, she had been to Kirkpatrick to plead, and he knew what a trial that must have been for them both. Indeed, Nita must have given up all hope if she had arranged for marriage.

Bitter laughter issued from his throat. The one thing above all else in life he had wanted was to be his on the eve of his death. He and Nita would marry. But in such surroundings! Or perhaps they would be allowed to go to the warden's office, perhaps Nita wouldn't be forced to come to these grim gray halls of steel and stone. It would be good to hold her in his arms for a moment… a moment…. Once more his head dropped into his hands. His teeth clamped on his lip. His shoulders jerked once, twice, but no sound came from behind his locked lips.

The afternoon slipped by insensibly. The county clerk came to ask the necessary questions and a marriage license was issued. After dinner, the guard changed. Wentworth toyed with the

174

food, thrust the tip of his cigarette through the bars for the guard to light. The night guard was a wry little Irishman.

"How yuh making it, pard?" he grinned.

"Swell," said Wentworth. "Just swell." There was no bitterness in his voice. Nothing, in fact, but a vast emptiness. He paced, slowly, the short length of his cell. After the lights went out, he still went on moving slowly, slowly, cigarette following cigarette to the floor. He laughed sharply once. Hell, this was the eve of his wedding!

All along the line of death cells, he could hear restless pacing. There were seven men here awaiting execution. Wentworth knew that all over the prison men were moving restlessly like that. Tomorrow night, it would be even worse. The cell blocks would ring with mad shouts and cries of terror, filthy abuse. It was always like that when a man was to die. When the lights dimmed and the electric current from the dynamo went into the apparatus of the chair....

He stopped his pacing, stared wide-eyed at the guard outside the door. Why, the next time the lights dimmed, it would be to send that current through his own body....

For a moment, black panic stirred within him—panic such as he had never known before. The prod of fear. And then the tension left him again, and he smiled derisively at himself.

What, the Spider afraid? Surely, this was a better death than going down filthily before the slugs of gangster guns? He shook his head. No, it was not that he had not feared death before. It was merely that he had never gone into a battle in which he did not have at least a fighting chance. This time, he would have no chance at all. He would be thrust into a chair, as helpless as a steer driven to the slaughter pens. And then....

Damn it! He must stop such thoughts, or he'd go mad. He started his slow pacing again. Such thoughts were foolish. He was not, he *would not* be afraid of death. Nita should not find him afraid tomorrow.

He laughed suddenly. Suppose they should marry and then he contrived an escape? He'd bless the day that had brought him to prison. He laughed again, and the sound was so gay that the guard outside the door hunched close against the grating.

"Say, got a cigarette for a guy?" he asked. "They're damned good ones, from the smoke."

WENTWORTH PASSED one out. He was smiling to himself. They had examined a few of his cigarettes, to find if anything was hidden in them, but they did not know that certain ones in his package contained a narcotic. Yet, of what use knocking out the guard? None at all, unless he wanted to kill himself then. And he had no intention of doing that. He would not, he could not, give up hope until the last moment.

The guard lighted a harmless cigarette and Wentworth tucked another between his lips. Somewhere off in the distance a heavy bell gonged slowly. He counted the beats: twelve. He leaned against the bars.

"What's good for insomnia?" he asked, "that is, besides a strong and sudden dose of electricity?"

The guard's laughter was surprised out of him. He guffawed twice before he could check it. "Man," he cried. "You've got *nerve!*"

Wentworth smiled sourly down at his cigarette. "I understand the judge said something like that, too."

He lifted the cigarette to his nose and sniffed at it, looked at the guard. "Say, do you smell something funny? Rather sweet-ish?"

"Disinfectant," growled the guard.

Wentworth began to feel the pound of his heart in his throat. Dizziness made the dimly lighted hallway waver before his eyes. What the devil? Had he got hold of a narcotized cigarette by mistake? His knees felt lax and loose. He clung to the iron grating, gasping with a throat that felt squeezed. He saw the guard reel to his feet, take two stumbling steps and pitch forward on his face. Then his own knees gave way under him. Blackness crowded in upon his mind. He slid down the bars and pitched sideways to the floor. The sweetish odor was stronger.

THE BLACKNESS became a peripheral gray and through it came the rush of wind, and distant voices he could not understand. He tried to speak, but his mouth felt dry, his tongue swollen and thick. Something cool touched his lips and he swallowed. The gray retreated a little. Fuzzily, he lifted his hands to grasp the cup at his mouth, drink again. His hand touched another hand—small and cool and soft.

He opened his eyes, jerked erect. "Nita!" he cried. "Oh my God, Nita!"

She was seated beside him, smiling into his eyes. He flung a quick glance to right and to left. He realized then the origin of that rush of wind. He was in a car, his own car, the Lancia. In

177

front were the broad, competent shoulders of Jackson. On either side the dark country was reeling past.

Jackson jerked his head about in a quick grin. "Feeling better, sir?" Then he pulled his eyes back to the road.

Wentworth shook his head violently.

"You got me out of prison," he said slowly. "You got me out of prison!" He breathed quickly, deep breaths which drove back the blackness threatening again to overwhelm him. He said weakly. "In heaven's name, Nita, how did you do it? The last thing I remember was feeling dizzy, seeing the death watch fall down...."

She looked at him quizzically.

Abruptly he sat bolt upright. "I've got it! You gassed the whole prison. Narcotic gas!

Nita laughed a little. But when his arm went about her, she laid her head gratefully upon his shoulder and suddenly she was crying, her shoulders quivering, her whole body racked by sobs.

He patted her head, pressed a kiss upon her forehead. But he did not attempt to stop her tears. His mind was racing. They were out of Sing Sing, but probably the search was already on. Every road would be watched, every town... If they were caught, Nita—for helping him—would face....

"Where are we going," he asked sharply.

"Airport five miles west of here, sir," Jackson called back. "Cabin job already bought and waiting."

Wentworth frowned into the darkness. The Lancia would be found, of course, and then a watch set for the plane—if they succeeded in taking off.

178

Suddenly Jackson swerved from the main road and jounced into a woody lane, his lights cut to dim. The reduced beam flickered over the back of a parked automobile and the Lancia stopped. Nita straightened, face wet with tears, but her lips smiling.

"I've got a disguise in that car," she told him. "You and Jackson fix yourselves up. A mile further along this road is a deep water-filled quarry that would swallow a dozen Lancias."

Wentworth threw back his head and laughed. "Nita," he said, "Hereafter, you are the Spider. I am only your assistant. You plan better than I. I want to hear more about that narcotic gas idea."

"I didn't think of it," Nita admitted. "Professor Brownlee did."

She jumped out and hurried to the car ahead, while Wentworth opened the secret wardrobe behind the seat in the Lancia, and made quick work of disguising Jackson and himself.

"I'll have to get a less expensive car," he told Jackson as he worked. "I've destroyed at least a half dozen of these Lancias and they run into money after a while." Happiness welled up within him. There was much to do yet, but even this much of an escape seemed too miraculous for despair.

As Jackson set the Lancia smoothly in motion toward the quarry and destruction, Wentworth jumped out. With an irrepressible laugh, he climbed into the rear seat of the other car beside Nita, and gathered her close into his arms.

"Darling," he murmured against her mouth. "I thought surely, when they told me about our approaching marriage, that everything was lost. That you'd given up hope."

She laughed softly. "That's what I wanted Kirk to think.

Otherwise, I'm sure he would have warned the prison officials to be on their guards. And yet, Dick—Kirk will be glad you've escaped. I honestly think he might have committed suicide...." She told him something of the scene with Kirkpatrick, the previous afternoon. "I think I might have felt sorry for him, if I hadn't been so wrought up about us," she concluded.

JACKSON CAME striding out of the darkness ahead and took the wheel. Within ten minutes they were speeding over the smooth highway again.

Professor Brownlee fixed up some little gray blocks that looked like big cones of incense," Nita explained Wentworth's rescue. "When they were burned they gave off a narcotic gas. It was colorless and very heavy, he said. He got on the windward side of the prison in a tug boat and threw these gas bricks into the fire box. When we were sure the gas had taken effect on those in the prison, Jackson climbed over the wall and we got the warden's keys and carried you out. I gave you an antidote for the gas, but Professor Brownlee says the others will stay unconscious for four to twelve hours."

"The professor is a wonder," Wentworth said huskily. "It was a lucky day for me when I saved him from disgrace at the college.... By heavens! Four to twelve hours! It's possible the alarm hasn't even been given yet! Anybody who came through the neighborhood for quite a while would be knocked out!"

"They wouldn't be apt to be wearing gas masks, as we were," Nita admitted with a little laugh. "The air field is just over this next hill to the right."

Minutes later they climbed into the cabin plane, waiting on

an empty field. Side by side they dropped into their seats as the motor roared and the plane trundled bumpily across the field. Nita put her lips close to his ear. "I almost decided to wait until tomorrow night to rescue you—after the wedding," she said. "I'm going to compromise you one of these days, mister, and then maybe Jenkyns will get a shot gun and make me marry you."

Wentworth's arm tightened about her shoulders. But he did not look at her. He couldn't, just then. It was not often the bitterness of their sterile love swept over him so terribly.

"We're already up fifteen hundred feet," he said thickly. "This plane can certainly climb."

CHAPTER 18
A DARING PLAN

T HEY SANK the plane in the Hudson river and took a previously prepared motor boat to the shore. Nita returned with Jackson to her apartment and Wentworth vanished into the jungle of the great city. In his disguise of a redheaded erect young man with a brush of a red mustache, he walked into one entrance of the Pennsylvania terminal, suitcase in hand, out of the other and took a taxi to the Waldorf-Astoria where he engaged rooms, sent for all newspapers.

He turned to the front pages and read, with set lips and burning eyes, the history of recent days. Five men had been murdered by the Headsman in New York and Chicago, all of them prominent in industry and finance. Reading, he tried to puzzle out from his knowledge of interlocking companies and interests, just who was being benefited by these crimes. And his discovery pulled him up sharply in his chair.

According to the investigations of Ron Conley, whose papers Nita had turned over to him, all of these killings could be of especial help to one Ronald Taliaferro, gold mine specialist and brother of the missing Welver. For Conley's account of Taliaferro's holdings matched strangely with the list of Headsman killings!

Wentworth deliberately made these calculations before he turned to the main story of the paper, the story of the Neanderthal hordes and the terror they spread.

They had abandoned the central mountains of Kentucky, where they had first ravaged the countryside, and were moving toward the Mississippi river. Their wake was a strip of devastation. But the horde moved always at night, silently, without lights, and patrolling airplanes could not spot them. Soldiers thrown across their path either missed them, or found their own sleeping camps invaded by beast-men who could murder a sentry before he realized danger within a hundred yards.

Traps had been set, dynamite pits with delicate triggers. Some few of the beast-men had died that way, but their clever noses led them around most pitfalls. Towns went up in smoke, men and women were fearfully mutilated, until all along the banks of the Mississippi people were fleeing their homes. Great motorcades of them, household goods piled in their cars, fled before the onslaught of the hordes. It was a barbaric invasion such as America had never known, a sweeping advance of killers like that of the hordes of Attila the Hun.

WENTWORTH LET the papers drop to the floor and stared at the blank wall. He must strike swiftly, swiftly. While he had lain helpless in prison this horror had spread. His lips parted in a hard and menacing grin. There was a way. It was full of dangers, of opportunities for disaster, but it was a plan. If he struck boldly....

He crossed to the phone and called Nita. Jackson answered.

"Jackson." His voice snapped with authority. "Kidnap Tremaine James and take him to Horton, Kentucky, by airplane. You'll receive orders there. Let me speak to Miss Nita." When Nita came to the phone, he asked swiftly if she had heard from the police. When she told him they had not yet come to question her about his escape, he laughed shortly, tensely.

"Apparently, the Sing Sing break still hasn't been discovered," he said. "Nita, I want you to fly to Chicago. Jackson will join you there at the Blackstone hotel. Then you two will kidnap Oscar Hedley the financier, and bring him to Horton. I'm leaving for there at once. I'll take over when you arrive. I have a plan!"

An hour later, he was flying westward in a large cabin plane he had purchased outright. By the time the sun had reached its meridian, he was circling low over the hills of Central Kentucky. He set the plane down in a clearing, masked it with branches in the edge of the woods and hiked into Horton.

Around midnight Jackson set down a speedier ship at Paducah and Wentworth took charge of his prisoner, Tremaine James. Within an hour Jackson was on his way again. Meantime Ron Conley was busy in the backwoods near where the cabin plane had been left. He had Taliaferro captive in a vine-grown log cabin of ancient vintage. Late the following afternoon, Jackson returned and this time he and Nita alighted with a man who seemed almost an invalid. Although the weather was hot, the man was muffled to the eyes in a scarf and topcoat.

WENTWORTH HELPED him solicitously to an automobile and, Jackson at the wheel, they whirled away from the field. Wentworth turned to Nita. "Darling, I told you not to come. There will be danger...."

Nita smiled at him mockingly. "Who would have thought it?"

"All right," said Wentworth grimly. "Since you're here I'll have to take you. Did your friend here make strenuous objections?"

"Not too much," she said thoughtfully. "I gave him a shot of morphine three times on the way here. It's time for another if you want to keep him quiet."

Wentworth laughed shortly. "I'm in for a rough time of it when this affair is over. I doubt very much that the innocent men I have kidnapped will appreciate that it was all done in the service of humanity."

"Innocent men?" Nita was curious.

"I'm kidnapping three," Wentworth told her. "I don't see how more than two of them could be guilty. These three men, Hedley, Tremaine James—he's already at the cabin—and Taliaferro are the three men who stand to profit most from the criminality of the Headsman and the work of the Neanderthal horde."

They rode in silence, while the car skirted Horton and sped on into the hills. At the mouth of a rutted lane which led to a dilapidated old cabin, Wentworth halloo-ed. From behind the thick growth of trees came a faint answer. Presently he came in

184

sight of the cabin door. Conley stood in it, facing toward the dark interior. As Wentworth spotted him, he threw back his head and shouted again.

Softly, Wentworth edged from the underbrush and crept toward him. From ten feet away, he called softly to Conley.

"Don't shoot, Conley," he said. "What's the matter?"

Conley still did not turn his head. "Masters and Beth," he said. "They followed Taliaferro's trail here and think, now, they're going to take him away from me…."

Wentworth said, "That's fine. I was going to ask you to go back to town and get Masters. Now we're spared that trouble."

He slid inside the cabin. "Want to go with us peaceably, Masters, or shall we truss you up?"

"Who the devil are you?" Masters demanded angrily. "I know if you don't let me out of here at once, I'm going to take both of you apart with my fists." His red beard fairly quivered with his indignation.

Beth, Wentworth saw, was crouched hopelessly beside a gaunt, slab-sided man, Ronald Taliaferro. He was the mountaineer type, hard-jawed, keen-eyed. He chewed a large wad of tobacco nonchalantly.

Tremaine James sat in a forlorn huddle against the wall, his cherubic face bowed, his vest creased across his slumped round belly. He glanced up glumly at Wentworth's entrance.

"It looks," said Wentworth gently, "as if I'd better tie up Masters." He caught up a loop of rope and advanced toward where the other crouched. He had taken two steps when Masters came up from the floor like a coiled spring, fists flying.

Beth screamed and covered her face. Wentworth dodged the first wild punch, stepped inside Masters' guard and clicked his right fist against the man's bearded jaw. Masters' arched backward, hit on his shoulders and rolled over limply on his face.

WENTWORTH REVIVED Masters, strung all his prisoners together on a rope, and marched them down toward the automobile, Ron Conley stalking along behind the line. Conley had tried to walk with Beth, but she had fled from him, still weeping.

"What's wrong with Masters?" he asked swiftly. "He's been a damned good scout throughout this trouble. Beth… trusts him. About the only time we've beat off the Neanderthal men has been when he was with us, fighting."

"That is… interesting," Wentworth said slowly. "I'm going to give him another chance at the beast-men, Conley. I'm going to give all these gentlemen a chance in fact—after I catch Jack Hawks. Do you want to come along? If you don't, I'll have to ask you to keep Beth from talking about this."

Conley looked at him oddly, then said shortly, "I'll come. We'll both come."

A half hour later, Jackson lifted the big cabin plane off the ground with its load of five prisoners—Beth being along as an unwilling passenger—besides Nita, Wentworth and Conley, and turned the ship's blunt nose westward. The cabin was sound-proofed and the hum of propeller came through only dimly. Wentworth faced his four men prisoners.

"It shall be up to you gentlemen to decide where we shall land," he said cheerfully. "We're going out to overtake the Neanderthal horde. When we find them, we'll drop into their path and allow you gentlemen to hold consultation with them. The horde has crossed the Mississippi. Last night three towns were sacked and laid waste. Tonight, doubtless, other towns will fall under their attack. But we, the eight of us, are going out first as a sort of peace conference, to have a little talk with the beast-men."

Tremaine James' mouth sagged open. "But, good God, man!" he cried. "They don't know what a flag of truce is! They'll tear us to pieces!"

Wentworth lifted his brows. "Do you think so, Mr. James?"

Hedley raised his heavy, round head, with its bristling reddish hair. "Come on," he rasped at Wentworth. "Out with it. How much money do you want us to pay you?"

Taliaferro's nasal whine cut in before Wentworth could answer.

"He don't want money, gents," he said. "He's got some deeper game than that. What is it, young feller?"

Wentworth jerked a stiff bow in Taliaferro's direction. "Thank you sir," he said jauntily. "You are a gentleman of remarkable penetration."

Masters was staring savagely at Wentworth. All of them were seated, in the single seats of the cabin, bound back against the cushions. Nita had Beth Welver in the rear compartment. Conley stood at Wentworth's elbow.

"Listen, punk," Masters said heavily. "Who in the hell are you?"

Wentworth smiled at him. "Is that important?"

"Damned important," Masters growled. "I've got a hunch...."

"Yes?"

"I've got a hunch that you're... the Spider!"

Something like panic brushed the chubby face of Tremaine James. Hedley leaned forward against his bonds, glowering, and Taliaferro breathed in deeply, then let his harsh lips relax in a grin.

"The Spider," drawled Taliaferro, shifting his 'chaw.' "Well, well, that's interesting. I might almost say it was good news."

Wentworth shrugged. He turned his back on the men, carefully tacked on the forward wall a large map of the states west of the Mississippi. He took a long pointer and stood beside it, facing them once more.

"The three towns marked with red," he said slowly, "are the ones the Neanderthal beasts ravaged last night. Now then, I want suggestions from you gentlemen as to where they'll hit tonight. We're going to find out which city will be attacked next, and then you gentlemen are going out to talk with the beast-men."

CHAPTER 19
A STRANGE WARNING

NIGHT CAME slowly at five thousand feet. The earth was a dark featureless blur, the wide Mississippi glinting off to the east, but up here, the air was still filled with dancing yellow motes of sunshine.

Wentworth had spent the entire afternoon trying to worm

from one of his prisoners the point at which the horde would strike next. His efforts had been in vain.

He had lashed them with bitter words, but his tone carried his lack of determination. The head of all these fierce activities, if he were there, must have known full well that Wentworth would not act until he was reasonably sure which of them was the guilty one.

Taliaferro even told him that, after a while. For an instant Wentworth crouched over the wealthy mountaineer, half determined to beat knowledge out of him. Then he strode stiffly toward the rear where Beth Welver and Nita sat listlessly. Conley had given up arguing with her and sat at a window. Even the plane was dark now. Its lights blinked on. Wentworth stood staring angrily down at the dark earth, his hands clenched behind him in one white fist.

Still staring down, he stiffened abruptly as he spotted a light, blinking off and on at regular intervals. Was he crazy, or did those flashes spell out... S O S? By heavens, they did!

He darted along the narrow hallway between the seats where his prisoners were tied, ducked under the map, and stepped into the control pit behind Jackson.

"Circle," he shouted Grasping the switch to the running lights of the ship, he blinked them on and off, Morse code for a question mark. He left the lights off then, and peered down, seeking the point of blinking light. It began again, clicking on and off with expert rapidity.

B-E-A-S-T M-E-N A-T-T-A-C-K P-E-R-R-Y I-N

H-O-U-R W-A-R-N T-O-W-N

Wentworth called the letters in slow sequence as the light blinked on below. Perry was one of the towns in the area mapped. He balled his fists at his sides, then his hand flew to the light switch.

"OK," he signaled back. "Who are you?"

The light below blinked again. "H-A-W—" and then went dark. Wentworth cursed under his breath. Unless he was completely insane, that light below was spelling out Hawks and it had been stopped in the very midst of the signaling.

But why should *Hawks* signal a warning? Hadn't Hawks been with the beast-men in the raid on Coonville, hadn't he been on the point of shooting a man behind the barricade when Wentworth had spotted him? Hadn't he faked his own death with the help of the Headsman?

WENTWORTH SHOOK his head in bewilderment. Leaning over Jackson's shoulder he shouted directions, then he ducked back into the cabin of the plane again, mind still whirling with the implications of the light signals. Was it possible the horde had broken away from its master, and was running wild over the country? But even if that were so, would Hawks deliberately plot their destruction, sign his own name to the warning....

He stood glaring at his prisoners. "Gentlemen," he said, "I've found a landing place for our peace mission. We'll meet the horde of beast-men at..." he paused, glancing keenly over their faces... "at Perry."

If the name of the town meant anything to them, he did not discover it.

He flung angrily back into Jackson's compartment and busied himself with the radio, tapping out a warning that the beast-men would attack Perry. Before he got halfway through the message, he felt that the key was dead and bent anxiously over the instrument. His fumbling hands could not find the source of the damage.

"How far are we from Perry?" he asked.

"Half an hour anyway," Jackson called over his shoulder. "We're bucking a head wind and a strong one. What's up?"

Wentworth told him rapidly. "When you get a mile from Perry, drop some magnesium flares and pick out a spot to sit down. I want to land in the path of the beast-men and hold a conference with them." Once more he ducked back into the cabin, this time hurrying back to Nita. Rapidly he told her what he planned.

"As soon as we land, I want you and Beth to start for the town with Conley here, and warn them what's going to happen. Perry has about five thousand people. If they'll all get together in the brick or stone buildings and get all their arms together, they should be able to stand the beast-men off until they can get militia from some other nearby town."

"What are you going to do?" Nita asked quietly.

Wentworth smiled at her grimly. "I'm going to take my little party out to chin-chin with the beast-men. I had thought it would be necessary to spot the horde, catch Hawks, and bring him in to talk with the rest of the party, but now I'm beginning to think Hawks was all right I'm afraid something happened to him when his light went out. I believe we have all the persons necessary to make the party a success."

She caught his arm. "Dick, you aren't going to do that!"

He shrugged. "Don't be silly, dear," he said gently. "Unless I do, Perry will be wiped out, a thousand families will be driven from their homes, many killed."

Still her hand clung to his arm. "But, Dick," she said hesitantly. "You've done so much already… This is hopeless. It means death."

Wentworth laughed at her fears. But he had an inward feeling of cold that echoed her doubts.

He had fought many times before against great odds. He had gone into battle against other criminal hordes. But those had been men, who could know fear, who could be swayed by reason and doubts and pain. Tonight, he went against men who were little better than beasts. Men who had a fierce vitality that almost defied death. Men who could not be reasoned with, could not even be spoken to. And yet it had to be done.

It was not Perry alone that was threatened. It was half the western part of the United States. Perry was close to the foothills of the Rockies. Once let the Neanderthal men take root in those great mountains, parts of which even yet remained unexplored, and nothing short of an army could root them out. They would continue to foray over the countryside, striking terribly, in the night, at helpless towns… No, no, it must be tonight. He would not be entirely helpless.

He bent to kiss her, then strode forward again and faced

the four men who huddled miserably in their seats. Slowly he looked them over.

Taliaferro, Masters and Hedley were stern-faced, unrelenting. Hatred glared from the eyes of Masters and Hedley. Taliaferro's thin hard-jawed face seemed more passive, more at ease than any of the others. Constant tremors raced over the body of Tremaine James. Already he seemed to have shaken pounds off his chubby face. It was apparent that he had no stomach for physical dangers.

"In five minutes," Wentworth told them equably. "The plane will be put down in the path of the horde and we will walk out to meet them."

LITTLE WHIMPERING moans came from James. The others received the words in deep silence, though it seemed to Wentworth that Hedley's ruddy color had faded somewhat. Behind, the door was punched open so suddenly that the map ripped loose from the wall and fluttered to the floor. Jackson's strained white face showed. Wentworth stepped into the compartment with him and shut the door.

"What is it, Jackson?"

Jackson pointed wordlessly downward. A magnesium flare, attached to a parachute, was drifting toward the dark earth. It spread a ghostly blue-white brilliance over the landscape. By its light, Wentworth could see a solid flow of beast men, leaping, running, diving through the close shrubbery of the fields below.

"We're only a mile out of town, sir," Jackson said hoarsely. "We're too late."

Wentworth's eyes glinted. "I'll take over," he sharply. "Drop another flare."

Jackson slid out of the seat and he took the wheel-stick, watched a second magnesium flare float down, then shoved the stick forward. The whine of the engines mounted swiftly, the earth leaped to meet the ship. Below them, the beast-men scattered to left and right, plunged frantically into the woods and shrubbery as the great bird from the sky swooped toward them.

Three times Wentworth circled and dived and at the end of that time, not a beast-man was in sight. Then he shot the plane toward Perry, skimming the tops of the trees.

"I think it will take them some time to reorganize," he said in a flat, hard voice. "We should be ready by then."

The lights of Perry swooped toward them out of the darkness ahead. But there was no landing field on this side of the town, they found. A muddy, low river crawled along the northern outskirts and on both banks, the slatternly huts of negroes cluttered the roadside. A bridge there was arched over with steel.

"We can't land," Jackson said gloomily. "Those telegraph poles keep us from using the road. The bridge…."

Wentworth laughed sharply. "The poles are on only one side of the road, Jackson."

With the words, he cut the motor and the plane dipped. The earth was scarcely a hundred feet below its retractable landing gear now. Wentworth wobbled the stick a little to level off, and swept in on the road at an angle. When the plane was only twenty feet up, he fish-tailed to the left, came gliding in on the road with the right wing grazing a telegraph pole. A hundred feet before the wing would reach the next one, the plane's wheels just touching the road....

"Hold tight everybody!" he shouted.

The wing smacked the second pole and the plane, all three points solid on the ground, wheeled sharply to the right. It bounded over a ditch and tossed its tail high in the air. The lights went out. But the plane stopped like that, its nose resting on the ground. Wentworth climbed out of the pilot's seat and spewed the beam of a pocket flashlight behind him. Jackson was clinging to two crash straps, smiling back at him.

"Nice landing, sir." The two fought their way up the steep slant of the aisle until their combined weight forced the tail down to earth. Wentworth turned, helped Nita and Beth Welver to the ground. Then he shouted through his cupped hands.

"All out for the peace conference!" There was an ugly mirth in his voice. He and Jackson, guns in hand, untied the complaining prisoners from their seats and, leaving their hands manacled, ushered them from the plane.

"Get across the bridge and warn the town," Wentworth told Nita swiftly. "Beth, go with her. Conley, it's up to you to protect them. Beast-men may already be in the town."

Nita hung back, looking up into Wentworth's face. "Beth and Conley can give the warning," she said. "I'll stay."

WENTWORTH STARED down into her face and cursed softly under his breath. Nita's face was set. No amount of arguing would sway her.

"Off with you, Beth, Conley," he shouted. "Get to town and warn them the beast-men are within a mile of the city."

Conley protested but yielded to insistence and Wentworth handed Nita a heavy rifle, picked up a canvas sack and slung its loop over his shoulder, then clasped an automatic in each hand.

"Jackson, take off their handcuffs," he ordered. "Nita, keep this light on them."

He waited tensely while the manacles were taken off the four men, then he marched them to the middle of the road. There was a sharp driving power in his voice as he ordered them on.

"Peace conference, march," he jeered. "You may sing Onward Christian Soldiers if you wish."

They made a thin straggling line in the brilliant rays of the flashlight, as they walked along the concrete road. Taliaferro and Hedley walked stalwartly, heads up, arms swinging, backs stiff with anger. Tremaine James whimpered and trotted along on short, chubby legs scarcely able to support him. Masters, now and again, gave him a helping hand. Masters, of all the men, seemed least disturbed. He kept his chin with its bristling red beard pointed straight ahead and did not deign to look back at any of their captors.

Wentworth's mouth was rigidly set. He was staking everything on a long line of conjecture, staking his life and Nita's and those of innocent men on a chance that his thoughts had run absolutely true. But, damn it, he had to be right! He had to stop this march of the beast-men now, or years of warfare and suffering and death lay ahead. There was, too, the matter of his conviction for murder. He had to upset that also. If only Nita had not insisted on coming along! There had been no time for argument. One glance at her set face had been enough.

On and on, the struggling line of men marched. Any moment now they should sight the first of the beast-men, running along with animal-like trot, swinging great spears and devastating clubs… Wentworth holstered one automatic, reached into the canvas bag at his side and drew out a torch of wood and oil-soaked cloth. He lighted it between cupped hands, then strode on with the flame flickering and leaping about him.

Masters turned his head and stared at him curiously once, then looked forward again. The red-bearded adventurer walked with an arm about James' shoulders protectively. The other two men still walked alone.

Abruptly, Wentworth halted his little detail, harshly ordered silence. He listened, straining his ears through the summer night. From the roadside ditch came the threnody of night insects, then….

His lips tightened coldly against his teeth. He was aware of Nita shrinking more closely to him. Off there in the darkness ahead, a beast-man's scream had arisen, hoarse, challenging and terrible.

CHAPTER 20
WHEN THE HORDE CAME

THE FOUR prisoners stood rigidly. James still leaned on Masters. All of them stood staring into the darkness ahead. The scream was not repeated, but Wentworth knew the horde was drawing near. Within minutes it would be upon them.

"Jackson," he called. "Take Masters ten paces up the road."

Masters whirled furiously, but before the menace of Jackson's steadily held revolver, he retreated to the spot indicated. Wentworth faced the men who remained.

"Gentlemen," he said. "One of you can stop these beast-men from harming us. Unless you do it, I'm afraid all of us are going to die rather horribly within a very short while."

James dropped on his knees. "For God's sake," he whimpered. "For God's sake, don't be a fool, Spider. We... I know nothing. Take us away before it's too late."

The other two stared at Wentworth stonily.

"Is this why you've brought us here?" Hedley demanded bitterly. "To die because of your fool ideas?"

Taliaferro grinned slowly. "I reckon it ain't such a fool idea," he said. "Unless he forgot to bring along the guy what can boss them beast-men."

Wentworth met his grin with a confident smile of his own. "The guilty man is here, Taliaferro," he said. "You three men are the only ones who could possibly benefit from the series of murders the Headsman and his associate on the West Coast have been committing. Masters is the tool. One of you three is the master. It's pretty plain, with Perry under fire tonight, that the beast-men are being headed toward the gold mine district. You'd profit from that, wouldn't you, Taliaferro?"

"You mean if a lot of gold miners was killed?" Taliaferro asked, "and I got a chance to buy out from their kin? People scared off, willing to sell cheap? Things like that?"

"You've got the idea," Wentworth told him grimly.

"Well, now, I reckon you're right, mister."

Hedley was staring at Taliaferro with harsh commanding eyes, "If you're the fool who's turned these Neanderthal men loose on the country," he said, "I'll give you a million dollars to turn them back. You can have them kill this fool who brought us here."

Taliaferro spat speculatively toward the ditch. "Well now," he said, "that's a right nice figger. I reckon I'd like to take you up on that—" he grinned broadly, showing discolored teeth "—if so be I was the man."

Hedley cursed. His fists were clenched at his sides, there was a tension about his neck. James was on his knees, sitting on his heels, his head sagging. Now and again, his shoulders trembled convulsively. Wentworth looked at him speculatively. Taliaferro was a cool one. He had the backbone for such an enterprise as this. Hedley was sufficiently coldblooded, self-centered. Tremaine James....

Another roaring scream sounded in the darkness. It was much nearer. James started to his feet with a little choked scream, crouched shivering, looking from one side to the other. Wentworth was conscious of Nita close beside him, but the beam of light she held was steady. He took the canvas bag off of his shoulder and laid it open at his feet.

"The beast-men are getting pretty close, gentlemen," he said gently. "Don't you think one of you had better speak up?"

Hedley began to swear in tight, low monosyllables. Taliaferro continued to grin. He patted James on the shoulder reassuringly and the chunky little financier leaped a full yard in fear.

"How much longer," Masters called, "are you going to keep

Wentworth's automatic smoke, and Masters' mouth remained open.

up this nonsense?" There was no fear in his voice, but there was anger and strain.

Wentworth did not answer him, but James turned his head that way and stared fixedly at the two men in the shadows ahead along the road, Masters guarded by Jackson. Masters shouted again, his voice edged with excitement.

"You fools! I can see one of them!" he cried. "He isn't a hundred yards down the road. They can throw those spears fifty yards and send them clean through your body...."

WENTWORTH NODDED. "They're handy with those hammers, too," he said lazily. "One blow and your skull looks like bone meal. A bit more moist of course." James darted toward the roadside ditch with a little squeal and Wentworth sent a bullet digging the concrete at his feet. James stopped and at Wentworth's polite remonstrance came back. He kept glancing excitedly to left and right, into the darkness. "Tell Masters, James," Wentworth said gently.

The little man whirled to face Wentworth, his face white as paper, his eyes bulging.

"You know, James," said Wentworth, still softly, "that you engineered the Headsman kills, that you started all this horror in Kentucky. You are the man...."

As Wentworth spoke, the trembling in James' body ceased and he straightened with an effort. Hedley and Taliaferro stared at him with narrowed eyes.

"For God's sake," Masters' voice rose thinly, "do something back there. I don't...."

Wentworth saw him throw himself violently aside and heard

a spear grate on the concrete, saw it bounce into the air and come slithering down the middle of the road. It stopped within five feet of Tremaine James, its point directly toward him.

James shrieked and fell again on his knees. "Masters," he shouted. "Masters. Stop them. We can get rid of...."

Wentworth laughed softly. "Taliaferro, would you mind collaring that rat for me?"

Up ahead, Masters was booming out weird sounds that were guttural and almost formless. Sounds that must be words, for out of the shadows came answering grunts and howls that mimicked his own.

"Bring Masters here, Jackson," Wentworth called. Taliaferro had James by the throat, digging his thumbs into the tendons back of his ears. Now and again he shook him gently. The grin was still on the mountaineer's face, but it was hard and menacing now.

As Masters and Jackson came steadily toward them, shadows began to emerge from the darkness, great hulking, beast-like shadows. The Neanderthal men. They carried their spears threateningly, swung hammers gently to and fro in their hands.

Wentworth held the torch low in front of him and through its gleam, he stared at the beast figures that seemed to shy from the light. Masters suddenly began to shout more of the booming sounds, and from behind and from both sides, the beast men closed in.

"Wentworth," Masters was sneering, "unless you want the girlfriend there to become the general property of the tribe, you'd better throw down your guns. I'm going to kill you and this lad Jackson. I suppose Taliaferro and Hedley will have to go, too, but I'll see that the girl lives, and doesn't become tribal property, if…."

"My dear fellow," Wentworth interrupted quietly. "The moment one of the tribe makes a move toward me or toward my party, I am going to shoot you three or four times through the stomach. I'm afraid that what happens afterward will not be of much interest to you."

Masters laughed, said clearly, "There's a beast-man just behind you, with a throwing stone ready. If I even frown at you, he'll brain you. Don't forget that, if I die, all of you die also, but the young lady… not so slowly."

"You couldn't turn a woman over to those beasts!"

Masters sneered. "So you really think not?" There was a hard, cruel gleam in his eyes and his lips were apart, twisted nastily. "Wentworth, drop that gun!"

WENTWORTH SEEMED to hesitate. "Listen," he said. "I'll make a deal with you. I'll let you go free if you'll turn James over to me. He's the man who framed that Glastonbury murder charge against me, and he's really the man I want."

Tremaine James fear had slowly left him. He laughed now. "Surely, I framed you," he said, "and a sweet job I did of it, too. But you won't put over that sort of deal, Wentworth. I've still got most of the money and Masters knows which side his bread is buttered on."

"You framed me for murder," Wentworth cried. "You admit that!"

"Surely, I'll admit it, all the good it will ever do you," James said.

Wentworth turned gravely to Hedley and Taliaferro. "You heard what he said, gentlemen, that he framed me for murder." Taliaferro was still smiling. He spat again into the shrubbery. "Shore," he agreed, "but, like he says, what good is that going to do you?"

Wentworth laughed. He thrust the blazing torch down into the canvas sack at his feet, stepped just beyond it and pulled Nita there, too. Little blue flames licked up within the bag.

"It will do a great deal of good, gentlemen," Wentworth said. "Masters, if you open your mouth, I'll shoot you down."

Masters stared at him, narrow-eyed, then he opened his mouth and the beginning of a great guttural cry formed in his throat. Wentworth's automatic spoke and the mouth stayed open, but no further sound came from it. Nor was there any wound where the bullet had entered. Masters swayed, pitched stiffly forward and then it was possible to see where the bullet had struck. It had gone in his mouth and blown off the back of his head.

A bestial roar sounded from the darkness. And then Wentworth flung high his hands. From his throat boomed guttural sounds, the exact duplicates of those Masters had first flung into the darkness, those that had stopped the attack of the beast-men. The blue flames in the canvas bag were brighter now, blowing away from their own huddled group.

Wentworth began dragging out from his pockets small chem-

205

ical masks which would just cover mouth and nostrils. He passed those rapidly around.

"Put these on," he said swiftly, "and these beast-men will soon be out of the fight."

He clapped one over his own face and stooped above the canvas sack, lifted out a gray cone of solidified powder that weighed perhaps a half pound. He held its point in the blue flames until it caught, then tossed it just beyond and upwind of the ring of beast-men.

"If you other gentlemen will do the same on all sides…" he urged. He threw back his head, pulled aside the mask, and once more boomed out the sounds that Masters had made. Quickly he replaced the mask, his senses reeling. He watched the others hurl the burning cones out into the darkness. A dozen beast-men within his sight were already stretched out on the ground.

Nita's eyes were smiling up at him. The canvas bag was empty and, with a wide gesture, Wentworth motioned the party to turn toward the town. Taliaferro would not let go of James' neck and they stumbled along that way until they met a group of cautious riflemen marching out from the city behind Beth Welver and Roy Conley. Wentworth took off his mask.

"You'll find the beast-men back there, all dead to the world," he told them. "Tie them up. I wouldn't be surprised if you could sell them to the scientists and the zoos for as much as a thousand apiece."

The leader of the riflemen stared at him with bulging eyes. "A thousand dollars apiece?"

Wentworth nodded. "Yes, and they're all lying unconscious

back there from a narcotic gas invented by a friend of mine, Professor Brownlee. You'd better wait a half hour before you go much closer."

THE PARTY took up their trek toward Perry, Beth and Conley turning back with them. Taliaferro walked strongly ahead, thrusting Tremaine James before him. Hedley strode along pensively, hands clasped behind his back. When they had reached the plane once more, Wentworth called a halt and requested them all to listen for a few moments.

"Mr. Hedley, and you, Mr. Taliaferro. I want to apologize to you gentlemen, both for my suspicions and for my behavior toward you. What I did was illegal, dangerous and desperate, I admit. The only extenuation I have to offer is that—" he waved his hand back along the road—"the Neanderthal horde will no longer menace the American people, nor devastate its towns. Mr. Hedley, I suspected you because you were one of the backers of Hawks' expedition which found these beastmen. However, Hawks signaled from the earth tonight that the horde was going to attack Perry. By that, he made amends for many misdeeds. His message broke off in the midst. I'm afraid he was killed…" Wentworth paused. "I know now that Tremaine James tried to throw suspicion on Hawks by an obviously faked murder of Hawks while I was in his house. He kidnapped Hawks, intending to fasten all blame on him in the end when, if his fake of murder had not been discovered, the fake would add to suspicion against him. Hawks got free tonight, signaled when he saw my plane's light.…"

He paused again, met Taliaferro's dour glare, Hedley's unmoved gaze, and shrugged.

"If you gentlemen wish," he said, "you can send me to prison for a long term for abducting you—or rather ordering your abduction."

Hedley said grimly. "You took the words right out of my mouth."

Taliaferro nodded, spat out of a broken window of the plane. "You shore didn't win any right to ask no favors," he said.

Wentworth shrugged. "At least you'll be willing to testify that Tremaine James admitted his crimes, and that he admitted framing me for a murder I didn't commit."

Hedley nodded. "I don't see how we can very well help doing that," he said, "in common justice."

Taliaferro shoved James into a comer and sat down comfortably, stretched his long legs out to block his prisoner into the corner.

"Ron Conley," he said slowly, "you used to be sheriff. Reckon you could take this fella Wentworth in hand until we can get to a regular sheriff?"

Conley said, "You're fools. Both of you are fools. Wentworth is the finest man that ever lived. Without him, there'd be thousands more people killed. If James hadn't put him in prison, he'd have stopped all this long ago."

Taliaferro opened his keen gray eyes very wide. "You mean you won't do your bounden duty, Sheriff Conley?" he said.

Beth Welver was standing angrily beside Ron Conley. "He… Mr. Wentworth showed me the truth about Ted Masters. He's nice. If Ron Conley does arrest him, I'll… I'll never speak to Ron again!" she cried, "Nor you either, even if you are my uncle."

Taliaferro threw back his head and guffawed. "Well, I reckon that settles it. I ain't goin' to have my niece not talking to me. Looky here, Hedley, this guy Wentworth did do a good job of it. There was a little deal you've been wanting to put over about Lacawanna Lode. Now, 'spose I was to say I'd swing my votes your way…."

Hedley's face relaxed a little. "It's a deal, Taliaferro," he said gruffly, "but to tell the truth I didn't have any idea of pressing that charge." He coughed behind his hand. "I just thought this young fellow needed a bit of scaring."

Taliaferro gulped, made a wry face. "Scare him. Scare *him*. Listen, Hedley, next time you gonna crack jokes like that, let me know. I swallowed my tobaccy."

Wentworth laughed joyously. And Nita ran forward and threw her arms around Taliaferro's neck. "You're an old dear," she cried.

Hedley coughed again behind his hand. "I'm quite sure," he said, "that I'm at least ten years—ahem—*older* than Taliaferro."

POPULAR HERO PULPS AVAILABLE NOW:

THE SPIDER

❑ #1: The Spider Strikes	$13.95
❑ #2: The Wheel of Death	$13.95
❑ #3: Wings of the Black Death	$13.95
❑ #4: City of Flaming Shadows	$13.95
❑ #5: Empire of Doom!	$13.95
❑ #6: Citadel of Hell	$13.95
❑ #7: The Serpent of Destruction	$13.95
❑ #8: The Mad Horde	$13.95
❑ #9: Satan's Death Blast	$13.95
❑ #10: The Corpse Cargo	$13.95
❑ #11: Prince of the Red Looters	$13.95
❑ #12: Reign of the Silver Terror	$13.95
❑ #13: Builders of the Dark Empire	$13.95
❑ #14: Death's Crimson Juggernaut	$13.95
❑ #15: The Red Death Rain	$13.95
❑ #16: The City Destroyer	$13.95
❑ #17: The Pain Emperor	$13.95
❑ #18: The Flame Master	$13.95
❑ #19: Slaves of the Crime Master	$13.95
❑ #20: Reign of the Death Fiddler	$13.95
❑ *NEW:* #21: Hordes of the Red Butcher	$13.95

THE MYSTERIOUS WU FANG

❑ #1: The Case of the Six Coffins	$12.95
❑ #2: The Case of the Scarlet Feather	$12.95
❑ #3: The Case of the Yellow Mask	$12.95
❑ #4: The Case of the Suicide Tomb	$12.95
❑ #5: The Case of the Green Death	$12.95
❑ #6: The Case of the Black Lotus	$12.95
❑ #7: The Case of the Hidden Scourge	$12.95

G-8 AND HIS BATTLE ACES

❑ #1: The Bat Staffel	$13.95

CAPTAIN SATAN

❑ #1: The Mask of the Damned	$13.95
❑ #2: Parole for the Dead	$13.95
❑ #3: The Dead Man Express	$13.95
❑ #4: A Ghost Rides the Dawn	$13.95
❑ #5: The Ambassador From Hell	$13.95

CAPTAIN ZERO

❑ #1: City of Deadly Sleep	$13.95

OPERATOR 5

❑ #1: The Masked Invasion	$13.95
❑ #2: The Invisible Empire	$13.95
❑ #3: The Yellow Scourge	$13.95
❑ #4: The Melting Death	$13.95
❑ #5: Cavern of the Damned	$13.95
❑ #6: Master of Broken Men	$13.95
❑ #7: Invasion of the Dark Legions	$13.95
❑ #8: The Green Death Mists	$13.95
❑ #9: Legions of Starvation	$13.95
❑ #10: The Red Invader	$13.95
❑ *NEW:* #11: The League of War-Monsters	$13.95

DUSTY AYRES AND HIS BATTLE BIRDS

❑ #1: Black Lightning!	$13.95
❑ #2: Crimson Doom	$13.95
❑ #3: The Purple Tornado	$13.95
❑ #4: The Screaming Eye	$13.95
❑ #5: The Green Thunderbolt	$13.95
❑ #6: The Red Destroyer	$13.95
❑ #7: The White Death	$13.95
❑ #8: The Black Avenger	$13.95
❑ #9: The Silver Typhoon	$13.95
❑ #10: The Troposphere F-S	$13.95
❑ #11: The Blue Cyclone	$13.95
❑ #12: The Tesla Raiders	$13.95

DR. YEN SIN

❑ #1: Mystery of the Dragon's Shadow	$12.95
❑ #2: Mystery of the Golden Skull	$12.95
❑ #3: Mystery of the Singing Mummies	$12.95

MAVERICKS

❑ #1: Five Against the Law	$12.95
❑ #2: Mesquite Manhunters	$12.95
❑ #3: Bait for the Lobo Pack	$12.95
❑ #4: Doc Grimson's Outlaw Posse	$12.95
❑ #5: Charlie Parr's Gunsmoke Cure	$12.95